TO MARRY
McCLOUD

TO MARRY McCLOUD

BY

CAROLE MORTIMER

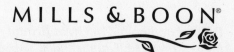
MILLS & BOON®

First published in Great Britain 2002
Large Print edition 2002
Harlequin Mills & Boon Limited,
Eton House, 18-24 Paradise Road,
Richmond, Surrey TW9 1SR

© Carole Mortimer 2002

ISBN 0 263 17370 4

Set in Times Roman 16½ on 17½ pt.
16-1102-48387

Printed and bound in Great Britain
by Antony Rowe Ltd, Chippenham, Wiltshire

CHAPTER ONE

'CELEBRATING?'

Fergus didn't even bother to look up from where he sat slumped in a corner of a noisy nightclub, staring down morosely into his champagne glass, totally removed from the loud music that played and the hundreds of chattering people that surrounded him drinking and smoking, and generally enjoying themselves.

What a stupid question; did he look as if he were celebrating?

'Has no one ever told you that you should never drink alone?'

Damn, the woman was still here! Couldn't she see that alone was exactly what he wanted to be? And how he intended on remaining, he mentally added vehemently.

'Mind if I join you?'

Of course he minded—

Wow...!

The woman's persistence had at least caused him to look up, the angry dismissal that had

5

rapidly been gathering force inside his head coming to a skidding halt.

This woman—girl?—was absolutely beautiful!

Barely five feet tall, she wore an above-knee-length fitted black dress revealing a slenderness, giving the impression she might snap in half at her tiny waist. Her hair was a long curtain down her delicate spine and the dark colour of midnight. Her face was ethereally beautiful, totally dominated by the deepest blue eyes Fergus had ever seen, and edged with thick, smoky black lashes.

So she was beautiful, was his next thought. So what? She was also pushy and forward, something he definitely did not need at this moment. If ever!

He leant back in the padded booth where he sat, his appraising gaze deliberately insolent as it moved from her head to her toes, and then back to that delicate china-doll face. He frowned. 'Are you sure you're old enough to be in here?'

She laughed huskily, revealing tiny, even white teeth. 'I can assure you, I'm well over the age of consent,' she told him in a cultured voice.

He wasn't aware he had asked her for anything! Couldn't she see that he wanted to be left alone, that he had been sitting here on his own for well over an hour now, that he had spoken to no one, and no one—wisely!—had spoken to him, either?

'Mind if I join you?' she asked again, indicating the seat in the booth opposite his own.

Yes—he minded! Did this woman have the skin of a rhinoceros? Could she really not see that he just didn't want to even speak to her, let alone anything else?

Obviously not, he decided frustratedly as, not even waiting for his reply, she slid smoothly onto the seat she had previously indicated.

'Look, Miss—'

'Chloe,' she put in smoothly, her blue gaze very direct as she leant her elbows on the table before resting that tiny pointed chin on her linked hands, staring unblinkingly across at him.

'Chloe,' Fergus echoed with an impatient sigh. 'I don't mean to be rude, but—'

'Then don't be,' she advised.

He had a feeling he was going to have to be if he wanted her to leave any time in the near future!

He sighed again. 'This has not been a good day for me, Chloe—'

'Maybe your luck is about to change,' she murmured.

He didn't *want* his luck to change!

He hadn't been looking forward to the wedding today—after all, it was the second one he had attended in a month. First his Aunt Meg had married restaurateur and chef, Daniel Simon, and today—much worse!—his cousin Logan had married Darcy Simon.

Not that Darcy wasn't a lovely girl, and he knew that she and Logan were head over heels in love with each other. It was just—he hadn't realised just how deeply Logan getting married was going to affect him. Since childhood, it had always been the three of them: Logan, their other cousin Brice, and Fergus.

They had grown up in Scotland, gone to university together at Oxford, had all remained single for the last fourteen years, not living in each other's pockets, but certainly enjoying the bachelor life when they had met. They had become known as the Elusive Three. Now there was only himself and Brice left. The Elusive Two just didn't sound the same...!

His mouth twisted wryly. 'I don't think so, Chloe. Thank you for the offer, but—'

'Would you like to dance?' she suggested lightly.

He wasn't even sure he could still stand up, let alone dance! The champagne had been flowing freely at the reception since the wedding ceremony this afternoon at three o'clock, and Fergus had definitely had more than his own fair share of the bubbly liquid.

When the party had begun to break up about eleven o'clock he hadn't felt he'd been ready to go home to his lonely house just then, instructing the taxi driver to bring him here instead. But at least he had had the sense to realise he had better stick to drinking champagne; otherwise he knew he would wake up in the morning wishing his head weren't attached to his shoulders. He still might!

He gave a heavy sigh. 'What I would like, Chloe, is for you—'

'Could I have some mineral water, do you think?'

He looked across at her darkly, wondering if she was ever going to let him get in a full sentence!

She smiled at him, and Fergus found his expression softening slightly. After all, it wasn't her fault he was in a foul mood. A mood that meant the last thing he wanted was to be so obviously approached by a woman he had never even seen before. Beauty notwithstanding!

'It's only a glass of water,' Chloe teased softly.

How right she was; he wasn't capable this evening of providing her—or any other woman, for that matter!—with anything else.

Okay, one glass of bubbly water, he promised himself, and then she would have to go.

He turned to signal the waiter behind the bar to provide him with mineral water and another glass, taking the bottle himself to pour some of the liquid for Chloe.

At least, that was what he intended doing, but at the last moment his hand seemed to have a will of its own, shifting slightly, some of the water spilling onto the table. Hell, just how much had he drunk today?

'Whoops,' Chloe sympathised gently, before placing a tissue over the spilt water. She raised her glass. 'What shall we drink to?' she encouraged brightly.

'Absent friends?' Fergus returned morosely before taking a huge swallow.

Not that he thought Logan would ever stop being his friend, as well as cousin. But he just knew things would never be the same between them now that Logan shared his life with his wife.

The same age, thirty-five, the three cousins had always been more like brothers, offering each other broad shoulders during times of trouble. It was going to take some time to adjust to the fact that Logan now had Darcy as his soul mate...

Chloe was eyeing him teasingly. 'I was always told that champagne should be sipped slowly in order to be properly appreciated.'

Fergus nodded tersely. 'Whoever told you that was correct.' Especially where a vintage champagne like this one was concerned! 'I did try to warn you I'm not very good company,' he glowered.

'So you did.' She appeared completely unperturbed by his taciturn mood. 'Is it anything you would like to talk about?' she encouraged softly.

Not to a woman he didn't know, and didn't want to know, either, thank you very much!

Chloe tilted her head thoughtfully to one side as she looked across at him, her hair taking on a blue-black sheen in the subdued lighting of the crowded nightclub. 'You're Fergus McCloud, aren't you?' she finally recognised appreciatively.

Fergus stiffened defensively. 'Am I?' he returned warily.

Was that the reason she had been so determined to speak to him? If it was, she was wasting her time; he wasn't into literary groupies. Again, beauty notwithstanding!

'Of course you are,' she answered. 'I've read several of your books, seen your photograph on the cover. You're very good,' she added warmly.

'Thanks,' he replied uninterestedly.

Chloe laughed. 'But you aren't impressed,' she easily guessed.

'Not really,' he returned bluntly. 'You see, I've read them too. They're your standard thriller: a bit of mystery, a touch of violence, mixed together with a lot of sex!'

'You've had six books published during the last six years, and each one has reached the number-one spot on the best-seller list,' she corrected softly. 'I would hardly call that ''standard''.'

Now, in spite of himself, he *was* impressed! But the fact that she knew all that about him only convinced Fergus more that this woman Chloe *was* a literary groupie. Or worse!

He shrugged. 'That just goes to show you that there's no accounting for public taste.'

'My, you are feeling sorry for yourself this evening, aren't you?' Chloe rejoined speculatively.

Yes, he was—so why didn't she just leave him alone to wallow in it?

Getting to know this man had turned out to be much harder than she had imagined it would be, Chloe admitted inwardly.

For weeks she had been desperately searching for a way in which she might 'accidentally' meet Fergus McCloud, finally coming to realise that it was virtually impossible. The fact that he was so successful as a writer meant that he no longer practised as a lawyer, so he didn't have an office to go to. His social life was sporadic, to say the least. The only thing she had been able to come up with, where she'd known he would definitely be in attendance, was his cousin Logan's wedding today; after all, he was the best man! But as Chloe didn't know either the bride or the groom, there was no way she could have gatecrashed!

Feeling thoroughly disheartened about the whole situation, she had accepted an invitation to spend the evening with a group of friends with whom she had been at university, going out to dinner before moving on to a nightclub. This nightclub. Chloe had hardly been able to believe her luck when, standing near the door with her group of friends and preparing to go on to somewhere else, she had actually seen Fergus McCloud coming in. Alone.

For a moment she had panicked, wondering what to do. Here had been her chance at last— and she hadn't known what to do about it! But then she had forced herself to calm down, to think.

The answer had been obvious; she'd made her excuses to her friends, explained she had changed her mind about going on somewhere else, and was going to go home. But, instead, she had followed Fergus McCloud back inside the club, standing at a discreet distance away to watch him while she'd decided what to do next.

He'd appeared to be alone, but she hadn't been sure whether or not someone, a woman, would eventually join him. After an hour, when he had drunk his way through one bottle of champagne, and ordered another one, she had decided that nobody would.

It was perfect, the ideal opportunity for her to at least have a chance to speak to him.

Except he had made it more than plain from the beginning that he didn't want to talk to her.

Well, she wasn't about to give up now!

'How did your cousin's wedding go today?' she enquired conversationally, making no effort to drink the water he had poured for her; it had only been a way for her to delay having him ask her to leave.

Fergus frowned across at her, his good looks not in the least diminished by his scowling expression.

Chloe had known what he looked like, of course, but even so she hadn't quite been prepared for the sheer physical force of the man. He was tall and powerfully built; there was no doubting he looked wonderful in his evening clothes. His dark hair was slightly overlong, his tanned face carved as if hewn from teak. Only his warm chocolate-brown eyes did anything to alleviate the hardness of his features.

Under any other circumstances, Chloe was sure she would find this man excitingly attractive. Under any *other* circumstances...

'I'm not sure I like the fact that you seem quite so knowledgeable about my private life,' he commented hardly.

That remark about his cousin's wedding had been a mistake, Chloe realised belatedly, laughing softly to cover up the gaffe. 'It's hardly a secret that the business entrepreneur Logan McKenzie is your cousin. Or that he was getting married today.' She shrugged.

'No...' Fergus conceded slowly.

But. He didn't say it, but the word was there in his tone, nonetheless.

Chloe drew in a softly controlling breath. She wasn't very good at this sort of thing, never had been. In fact, her behaviour this evening, approaching Fergus McCloud as she had, talking to him, inviting herself to join him, pressing him to provide her with a glass of water, was all totally out of character. Her friends and family would have been shocked if they could have seen and heard her! But she had been taken completely off guard by seeing Fergus arrive at the nightclub so suddenly, and had simply acted on impulse by inviting herself to join him. He certainly didn't look in a mood to introduce himself to her!

'It's the society wedding of the month, Fergus,' she chided him teasingly.

'Hmm.' He grimaced his distaste in recognition of that fact. 'Well, to answer your question, it went well. Or, as well as any wedding can be expected to,' he amended.

She raised dark brows. 'You don't like weddings?'

Once again he frowned across at her. 'You aren't a reporter, are you?' he prompted suspiciously. 'I'm not going to see my less-than-sober remarks splashed across the front page of a newspaper in the morning, am I?'

Hardly; she was no more enamoured of reporters than he appeared to be. They had already helped ruin her life once...

'No,' she assured him with certainty. 'I was interested, that's all.'

Struggling for a topic of conversation probably more accurately described it, she acknowledged ruefully. This was certainly heavy going.

'Well, as I've already told you, it was fine,' Fergus said abruptly. 'Now, if you'll excuse me?' He put down his glass, sliding over to the end of the seat in preparation of standing up. 'It's time I got myself a taxi home.'

Chloe stared across at him in dismay. He couldn't go! She hadn't even begun to talk to him yet. If he left now, she might never get the chance to talk to him again. This was—

'Oh, hell—!' Fergus McCloud groaned as, having attempted to stand up, he suddenly found himself sitting back down again. He closed his eyes, breathing deeply. 'I don't suppose you would like to do me a favour, would you?' he asked Chloe very carefully, his eyes still closed.

Anything! As long as it meant he wasn't about to just get up and walk away from her. Although, for the moment—thankfully!—he didn't seem able to do that.

'Yes?' Chloe responded breathlessly.

He continued to breathe deeply, looking across at her with those warm brown eyes. 'I seem to find myself temporarily unable to stand up. Actually, I'm drunk!' he amended with forceful self-disgust. 'Legless. Literally! I can't remember the last time I— Yes, I can,' he groaned. 'It was when I graduated from Oxford fourteen years ago. I couldn't get out of bed for two days afterwards!'

Her own graduation from university had only been a couple of years ago and, as she easily recalled, everyone had let themselves relax and had a good time; after three years' hard work, they had needed to.

'What would you like me to do?' she offered.

'Could you help me outside and put me in a taxi?' He grimaced. Obviously he wasn't a man accustomed to asking anyone for help.

She could do better than that, and it would suit her purpose much better. But she would keep that to herself for the moment...

'Of course.' She stood up smoothly, securing the strap of her evening bag on her shoulder before moving lightly round the table. 'Just stand up and lean on me,' she encouraged.

He eyed the slenderness of her frame with obvious scepticism. 'I don't think I had better ''lean'' too heavily,' he observed. 'Or we'll both fall over!'

He was a good foot taller than Chloe, even in her three-inch heels, and probably weighed twice as much as her too. But she was stronger than she looked, helping him to his feet without too much difficulty, her arm about his waist, his across her shoulders as the two of them began to walk towards the exit.

'This is so embarrassing,' Fergus muttered grimly when they had crossed half the distance to the door without mishap.

Chloe turned to grin up at him unsympathetically. 'Just think of it as practising for your old age!'

He gave a disgusted snort. 'I feel a hundred now!'

He didn't look it. In fact, he looked rather boyish, younger than the thirty-five years she knew him to be, his expression one of dazed disbelief at his own inability, dark hair falling silkily across his brow.

Chloe made no effort to put him into any of the waiting taxis once they were outside. Instead she helped guide him over to the green sports car in the adjoining car park, pressing the remote button on her keys as they approached to release the locks, swinging open the passenger door before helping him inside.

'This isn't a taxi,' Fergus finally realised, looking around him dazedly, the fresh air outside obviously having done nothing to clear his head. In fact, the opposite.

'No, it isn't,' Chloe confirmed as she got in behind the wheel to turn the key in the ignition.

Fergus looked ready to protest, and then thought better of it, leaning his head back weakly against the cream leather seat, his eyes once again closed. 'Whatever,' he accepted dismissively. 'Do I need to tell you my address—or do you know that too?'

Chloe turned sharply to look at him. Had she given herself away so completely?

Fergus opened one eye at her lack of response. 'Well?' he prompted impatiently.

She gave a slight inclination of her head. 'I know that too,' she conceded huskily, accelerating the car out of the car park and into the flow of late night traffic.

'Remind me, some time, to ask you *how* you know,' Fergus murmured drowsily. 'I have a feeling I'm not going to remember too much about this evening when I wake up tomorrow!'

Chloe sincerely hoped that wasn't the case...!

CHAPTER TWO

FERGUS woke slowly, totally disorientated for several long moments as he moved his head gingerly to look around what he recognised as the comfort of his bedroom, his head feeling as if it were full of cotton wool.

How had he got here?

Damned if he knew!

He glanced at the bedside clock. Nine-thirty. He lay back on the pillows, his eyes once again closed.

What day was it?

Logan and Darcy's wedding had been yesterday, he remembered that. So today must be Sunday, he decided. No need to worry about getting up just yet. He didn't have anywhere else to go, no one to see, and Maud, his housekeeper, always had Sundays off. He usually worked all day on a Sunday, grabbing a sandwich to eat if he felt hungry, so there was really no need for Maud to be here—

Then why could he smell coffee?

22

Champagne delusions? Because coffee was what he most felt in need of? As he had hoped, he didn't have a hangover, but his mouth felt as if it were full of sandpaper. A cup of coffee was very much on the agenda. He—

No, there was no doubt about it, he could definitely smell coffee. Strong, rich, reviving coffee.

But how—?

'Wakey, wakey, Fergus,' chirruped a bright female voice from somewhere over near the bedroom doorway. 'I've brought you up a mug of coffee.'

Fergus frowned, unmoving, eyes still closed, aware that the smell of coffee was much stronger now, but completely uncertain about the plausibility of that first statement. He couldn't possibly be awake. There was a woman in his bedroom.

Not that it was unknown for a woman to be in his bedroom; he had spent some very plea-surable hours with women in this four-poster bed. Just not last night. Not just champagne delusions, then, hallucinations, too!

'Come on, sleepyhead,' that female voice continued teasingly. 'Sit up and drink your coffee.'

Fergus slowly opened his eyes, wincing as he turned his head, half afraid of what he was going to see.

Deep blue eyes. A long cascade of blue-black hair. A slender female body obviously completely naked beneath his casually buttoned white evening shirt, the legs bare beneath its thigh-length.

Not hallucinations; he had to still be asleep. There couldn't possibly be an almost naked woman in his bedroom. He distinctly remembered he had left the wedding reception alone yesterday.

'Coffee.' She put down one of the mugs she carried on the table beside him. 'Black. No sugar,' she encouraged lightly.

Exactly how he took his coffee. But how did she know—?

'What are you doing?' he gasped disbelievingly as she sat down on the bed beside him.

She raised surprised brows, smiling down at him. 'You don't mind if I sit here and drink my coffee with you, do you…? Or that I borrowed your shirt to wear? It's cold downstairs in the kitchen.' She gave a slight shiver before taking a sip from her own steaming mug of coffee.

Fergus stared at her, not sure whether he wanted her to sit with him or not.

She had been roaming around the house, rooting around in the kitchen to find the makings of the coffee, obviously wearing nothing but his shirt! It was just as well it was Maud's day off! His housekeeper was perfectly aware of his bachelor lifestyle, but that didn't mean he had to flaunt it in her face.

Fergus turned away, ostensibly to pick up his own coffee and take a sip, but in actuality it was to give him a few more seconds' thinking space. Except that it didn't. By moving, he had discovered *he* was *completely* naked beneath the bedclothes!

Not that he should have been surprised by the fact, he realised dully. He didn't remember meeting this woman, didn't remember coming home with her, so why should he remember taking his clothes off?

There was, however, one undeniable truth to this situation: this woman—whoever she was—had obviously spent the night here. With him. In this bed. And he didn't remember a thing about that, either!

Not even her name…

How the hell had this happened? Too much champagne on an empty stomach, came the obvious answer.

He remembered leaving the wedding reception. He vaguely recalled going on to the nightclub. After that—nothing!

' ' 'Thank you, Chloe'',' she mocked behind him. 'You're welcome, Fergus,' she answered liltingly.

Chloe. Her name was Chloe, he acknowledged with some relief. But he didn't—

Yes, he did. Some of it was coming back to him now. The nightclub. She had come over and spoken to him. Sat with him, even though he had been less than enthusiastic. Had drunk with him. Gone to bed with him...?

Somehow he seemed to have missed something between drinking the champagne at the nightclub last night and waking up to find her in his bedroom this morning. He didn't remember the two of them going to bed together at all, let alone—let alone—

How the hell did he get himself out of this one? He groaned inwardly. One thing was certain: he was never going to drink champagne—or anything else!—to excess, again.

'Er—Chloe...?' He turned slowly, slightly more awake now, blinking dazedly as he took in this woman's delicate beauty.

She was so tiny. The hands that were cupped about her coffee mug were almost like a child's. Hands that were bare of rings, Fergus noticed with a certain amount of relief; at least he didn't find himself in this predicament with a married woman!

But that it was a predicament, he was in no doubt. How on earth were you supposed to behave towards a woman with whom you had obviously spent the night in bed—a night you didn't remember? An apology didn't seem to exactly fit the bill!

'It's good coffee,' he said inanely instead.

'Thank you,' she accepted warmly, putting her empty mug down. 'I simply can't tell you how wonderful it was to meet you last night, Fergus,' she added a little shyly

It was...?

Personally, he wouldn't have thought himself capable of giving of his best in the condition he had been in last night, but who was he to argue if she—?

Damn it, it wasn't a question of arguing; he simply didn't remember anything of being intimate with this woman the night before, and he could not pretend otherwise. But he could hardly tell her the truth, either, his conscience warned him softly. Not only would that be insensitive, it would be extremely insulting!

'I'm glad,' he answered noncommittally, absently playing with the dark silkiness of her hair as he wondered what to do next. 'Er—did we—?' He broke off as the strident noise of the doorbell ringing resounded through the house.

Someone was at the front door!

Obviously, you idiot, he instantly scorned himself. But who on earth could be calling on him at—nine-forty-five, the bedside clock showed—on a Sunday morning?

There seemed only one way to answer that question. But with the beautiful Chloe dressed in nothing but his shirt, Fergus was loath to get out of bed to go downstairs and answer the door. Maybe if he just lay here and ignored it, whoever it was would go away—

The doorbell rang again. Longer this time.

His caller wasn't going to just go away!

Chloe stood up. 'Shouldn't you go and answer that?' she prompted.

Of course he should. But it could be any-body: his mother, who was in town for the wedding yesterday, or one of the women he had taken out during the last couple of weeks. He could hardly introduce any of them to Chloe when he didn't even know who she was himself!

'Wait here,' he warned as he straightened, sitting up to swing his legs to the floor.

Yep, he was naked, all right. And a quick look round the room told him his dressing gown was in the bathroom where he had left it yesterday morning.

It was stupid to feel in the least self-conscious as he walked to the bathroom to get his robe. And yet he did. This woman might know exactly what he looked like without his clothes on, but *he* didn't *remember* her knowing. He obviously knew what she looked like without her clothes too, but he didn't remember that, either!

'I won't be long,' he assured her before leaving the bedroom, more relaxed now that he was at least wearing his robe.

What an awful situation. Who was Chloe? Where had she come from? More to the point, what was he going to do with her now...?

'Brice...!' he breathed hoarsely after opening the door and finding his cousin standing there on the doorstep grinning at him cheerfully.

'Fergus,' Brice greeted lightly. 'Nice car.' He turned to look appreciatively at a green sports car parked behind him in the driveway. 'Anyone I know?' Brice raised inquisitive brows.

Fergus stared at the car. He had never seen it before. For that reason alone he knew it had to belong to Chloe.

Well, at least that answered one of the questions that had been plaguing him since he'd woken up earlier and found her standing beside his bed; with a car like that she was unlikely to be someone who expected paying for whatever services she had provided last night!

'Or do I mean, anyone I should *like* to know?' Brice amended teasingly.

No doubt his cousin would be as knocked out by the way Chloe looked as Fergus was himself. But Fergus suddenly found that he didn't like that idea at all.

'What can I do for you, Brice?' he asked briskly.

The other man shrugged. 'Don't you remember that we made an agreement yesterday to play golf today? You said you weren't working today, so I've booked us in for a round at twelve o'clock,' he explained.

Golf. He had made arrangements to play *golf* today?

How on earth could he do that, when Chloe was still upstairs in his bedroom? When he had to find out exactly what—

'Good morning!' Chloe greeted cheerfully at that moment from directly behind him.

Fergus closed his eyes briefly in a wince. He had been hoping to put Brice off before going back upstairs to talk to Chloe; that way he could have avoided having the two of them meet. Her sudden appearance behind him meant it was going to be impossible.

'And a good morning to you too,' Brice returned lightly, looking past Fergus to smile at Chloe.

Fergus turned slowly, dreading the moment; Chloe had looked enchanting in his shirt, sexy as hell, actually, but, dressed like that, it was also obvious that she must have spent the night here. He and Brice were close, yes, but that didn't mean he wanted his cousin to see Chloe looking like that.

But he needn't have worried—she was completely dressed! The white shirt had gone, a short, slinky black dress in its place, her legs silky in sheer tights, high-heeled shoes on her tiny feet. Her hair was no longer tousled but brushed in a shiny blue-black curtain down the length of her spine, and her face was almost bare of make-up, except for a red lipgloss. But there was no doubt in Fergus's mind that she was the most exquisitely beautiful woman he had ever seen in his life!

She joined the two men at the door, her movements gracefully elegant. 'Aren't you going to introduce us, Fergus?' She looked up at him expectantly.

Introduce her to Brice? Yes, he supposed he better had. It was just that for a moment there her beauty had actually taken his breath away!

He took in a ragged breath, his arm moving lightly about her shoulders as he drew her to his side. 'Chloe, this is my cousin, Brice McAllister. Brice, this is Chloe—' He came to an abrupt halt, looking down at her frowningly. He had no idea what her surname was!

'Fox,' Chloe provided laughingly as she easily read his confusion, holding out her hand to shake Brice's. 'Don't mind Fergus, Brice; too much champagne!' she quipped. 'Now, if you'll both excuse me?' She included both men in the warmth of her gaze. 'I overheard you two say you're off to play golf, and I have an appointment myself at one o'clock. I obviously have to shower and change before then,' she added with a self-derisive grimace at her evening dress.

Obviously, Fergus acknowledged tautly, already wondering who this one o'clock appointment was with. Besides, she couldn't just disappear like this! When was he going to see her again? If at all?

Because suddenly Fergus found that he did want to see her again, very much so. It was very frustrating having this complete blank about their time together last night. He wanted to see her again, needed to see her—if only to have the chance to refresh his memory!

Chloe turned to him, smiling up at him before standing on tiptoe to kiss him lightly on the cheek. 'I'll ring you later, shall I?' she murmured discreetly.

The effect of that kiss on Fergus told him at least some of what must have happened to him last night; his cheek still tingled, and his insides felt as if they were melting.

He had dated some beautiful women in his time, some incredibly sexy ones too, but he could never remember reacting that strongly to a single, almost platonic kiss before. Chloe Fox was pure dynamite!

'Do that,' he confirmed abruptly.

'Nice to have met you, Brice,' she said with a nod before walking over to her car.

Fergus watched her go, admiring the lean grace of her body as she moved, her legs shapely as she swung easily into the low confines of the sports car, giving the two men a brief wave before reversing the car down the driveway and speeding away.

Brice whistled softly at his side. 'She's absolutely beautiful, Fergus,' he opined appreciatively.

She was gorgeous, Fergus mentally agreed. She—

She had just driven out of his life, he realised with a sickening jolt!

He, Fergus McCloud, a man who always ended relationships before they could possibly become serious, had just been given the brush-off. Big time!

Because Chloe Fox wasn't going to call him—she didn't have his telephone number!

Chloe managed to keep up her charade of cheerfulness until she had turned the corner away from Fergus McCloud's home. And then her knees began to shake, quickly followed by her hands, the latter so badly she was having trouble steering the car. So much so that she knew she had to pull the car into the side of the road, or end up crashing into something.

Leaning her head back against the leather upholstery, she closed her eyes as her whole body seemed to be shaking now.

She had forced her company on Fergus McCloud last night with the sole intention of talking to him, had driven him home for the same reason. Having him collapse unconscious on the bed as soon as she'd got him up the stairs had not been part of her plan!

She had stared down at him frustratedly for several long minutes as he'd lain on the bed gently snoring, knowing that if she'd left then, as he had already predicted, along with nearly everything else about last night, he wouldn't remember meeting her, either!

Having got that far, she hadn't been able to allow that to happen. And so she had stayed, curled up uncomfortably in the bedroom chair, while Fergus McCloud had slept the sleep of the untroubled in the huge four-poster bed!

It had seemed like a good idea at the time; now she wasn't so sure... She had aroused his curiosity, of that she was certain—he had obviously been stunned to wake up and see her in his bedroom this morning! But it was his compassion she really wanted. The problem was, she still wasn't sure he was capable of it...

And then his cousin had arrived so precipitously this morning, putting an end to any chance she might have had of talking to Fergus!

She drew in a ragged breath, having finally stopped shaking enough to turn on the ignition and continue the rest of the drive to her home. A home she shared with her parents.

What would Fergus McCloud make of that if he knew? No doubt, on the evidence he had from last night, he thought her a completely free agent, able to come and go as she pleased.

She hadn't missed that quick glance he had given the ring finger on her left hand, had easily seen him relax when he'd discovered no wedding band there. But to assume she was answerable to no one just wasn't true.

Although she should be in luck this morning; her parents should have gone to church by now, leaving her free to enter the house undetected.

She parked her car in the driveway beside her mother's car, her father obviously having ferried them to church in his four-wheel drive.

Chloe breathed a sigh of relief, knowing that if her parents saw that she was still wearing the dress she had worn to go out in the previous evening, they would guess immediately that she hadn't been home all night. And the last thing she wanted were any questions concerning her whereabouts previously!

She had reached the bottom of the wide stairway to go up to her bedroom, completely undetected by any of the household staff, when a door suddenly opened behind her.

'Chloe…?'

David. Her brother-in-law, and also her father's assistant. It could have been worse!

She turned to smile at him. 'Don't you have a home to go to?' she joked, knowing that her sister, Penny, and their three children would be waiting for him there. And this was Sunday, after all...

Tall, and sparely built, his blond hair thinning slightly on top, David Latham had been her father's personal assistant for the last fifteen years.

His presence in the house had brought him into close contact with all the family, and twelve years ago he had married Chloe's older sister Penny. Their parents had been thrilled at the match, and absolutely doted on their three grandchildren: Paul, aged ten, named after his grandfather, Diana, aged seven, and five-year-old Josh.

'I just had to stop by and drop off some papers your father needed as soon as he gets back from church.' He held up the papers. 'And shouldn't I be the one asking if you forgot last night that you have a home to go to?' he drawled, eyeing her clothes pointedly. 'I'm pretty sure you aren't going to join your parents at church dressed like that!' he added forthrightly.

'You would be right,' she grimaced.

'Don't look so worried, Chloe.' He laughed softly. 'I was young once, too, you know.'

David obviously assumed she had been on a raucous night out. And it would be better for everyone if he continued to think that.

'I won't tell my father about you if you don't tell him about me,' she returned lightly, knowing that, right now, given her father's precarious political position, appearances were everything, including those of his son-in-law and assistant, as well as his youngest daughter. 'Now I think I had better go upstairs and shower and change—before anyone else sees me!'

David grinned. 'You look as if a little sleep mightn't come amiss, either.'

He was right, Chloe discovered a few minutes later on looking in the dressing-table mirror in her bedroom. There were dark shadows beneath her eyes, and her cheeks were very pale too.

But it had been a long night. Most of it, she remembered, spent sleeplessly as she'd sat in that chair in Fergus McCloud's bedroom, wondering what sort of man he really was.

Oh, she knew his background. Knew Fergus and his mother had gone to live in his Scottish grandfather's castle after his parents had divorced, that he had gone on to become a lawyer after university, that his career had been put on a back-burner since his rise to stardom as a writer six years ago. But those weren't the things she needed to know about him...

Was he a kind man? A compassionate man? A man who believed in fairness, even at a cost to himself?

Those were the things she needed to know about Fergus McCloud—before she could even begin to ask him for what she really wanted from him.

Contrary to David's advice, she didn't go to bed, lunching at home with her parents, and David, Penny, and the children would join them, as they usually did on a Sunday.

Chloe spent the afternoon with her mother answering letters, and accepting or refusing the numerous social invitations they had received during the week. Where possible they were accepted; her father was about to make a political comeback, and being seen socially was necessary to that campaign.

But thankfully there were only the three of them at home for dinner this evening, meaning they could eat more intimately in their family dining-room, rather than the much larger room they used when they had the numerous guests that were invited to dine here at least once a week.

The meal was superb, as usual, but by the time they had been served and eaten dinner Chloe was definitely feeling the effects of her lack of sleep from the night before, excusing herself as her parents lingered over their coffee and brandy.

'You're looking a little pale this evening, darling.' Her father looked up at Chloe concernedly after she had bent down to kiss him goodnight.

He was tall, handsome, and distinguished-looking, at fifty-five, his dark hair only showing faint tinges of grey at his temples. Chloe absolutely adored her father, would do anything in the world that she could for him. Anything!

He was infinitely kind, his compassion all consuming. He always thought of others before himself. In fact, he had all of the attributes Chloe was hoping to discover in Fergus McCloud!

She felt a heaviness in her chest just at the thought of the other man. He was another one of the reasons she was going to her bedroom earlier than usual. She had been putting off telephoning him all day, partly because she felt a certain apprehension, but also because she hoped it would make him more curious about her when she did eventually make the promised call.

Until she knew Fergus a little better, and could gauge the best way to approach him, she wanted to keep him guessing where she was concerned.

And she had certainly done that this morning! It was probably extremely naïve of her, but it really hadn't occurred to her when she'd made the decision to stay last night that Fergus would believe the two of them had spent the night together in his bed. One look at his face this morning and she had known that was exactly what he had thought!

'I had rather a late night,' she answered her father ruefully.

'Then an early night today is the ideal thing, darling,' her mother encouraged warmly as Chloe kissed her goodnight.

Also in her mid-fifties, her mother was still very beautiful. She was tiny, with dark shoulder-length hair; her face was youthful, almost unlined, and her figure still as slender as when she had been Chloe's age. Her deep blue eyes were always full of warmth and kindness. And never more so than when she looked at her younger daughter.

Penny had already been ten when Chloe had been born, a rather late surprise for all of them. But even as a very young child Chloe had sensed she was all the more precious to them because of that. As her family, and their happiness, were now infinitely precious to her...

'I'll see you both in the morning.' Chloe's smile included them both, that smile fading as soon as she was out in the hallway. Much as she would like to, she really couldn't put off telephoning Fergus McCloud any longer...!

Once in the privacy of her bedroom, she took out her mobile phone and dialled his number—before she could change her mind! If she thought about it too long, she simply wouldn't do it!

She felt her heart sink as the number kept ringing and ringing. It had never occurred to her that he wouldn't be at home when she did decide to ring him!

What—?

'Fergus McCloud,' came the sudden abrupt response as the receiver was finally picked up the other end.

Chloe drew in a controlling breath before answering. 'Have I interrupted something?' she enquired with a husky confidence she was far from feeling. But it wasn't going to help her cause if Fergus knew she had been so nervous about making this call and talking to him that she felt physically sick!

There was a brief silence on the other end of the line, and then, 'Chloe...?

He sounded uncertain, less sure of himself than he had last night and this morning. Perhaps the waiting game had worked after all...?

'Who else were you expecting?' she came back. 'Or is that a silly question?' After all, he could have a woman—several women!—in his life.

The enquiries she had made about him discreetly the last couple of weeks hadn't uncovered too much concerning that side of Fergus's private life. Although it seemed he hadn't gone to his cousin's wedding yesterday with a companion, otherwise he wouldn't have been on his own last night at the club. Would he...?

'Not at all,' he drawled, sounding more re-laxed now. 'Actually, I was in the bath when the phone rang; I had to get out to answer it.'

But he didn't sound too put out by that fact... 'Does that mean you're standing there completely naked even as we talk?' Her tone was deliberately provocative.

Which was far from the way she was actu-ally feeling! Just the thought of it conjured up visions of last night and this morning, of Fergus, in all his naked glory, strolling casu-ally across the bedroom in order to get his robe from the bathroom.

It had taken every ounce of will-power she possessed not to turn away, to act as if she thought nothing of his nudity!

Although, she had to admit, Fergus was well worth looking at. Tall and muscular, his skin lightly tanned, not an ounce of superfluous flesh on his body, he moved with a lithe grace that was almost feline.

'Not exactly,' Fergus answered dryly.

'Oh.' She sounded disappointed.

'I'm sitting down, actually,' he corrected laughingly. 'And I'm getting rather cold too,' he added uncomfortably.

'Mobile phone,' Chloe told him abruptly—in order to stop her thoughts dwelling too long on those memories of his physical attributes.

'I beg your pardon?' he came back in a puzzled voice.

'If you had a mobile phone, you could take it into the bathroom with you,' she explained self-consciously.

'No, I couldn't,' Fergus assured her firmly. 'I hate the damned things. They're an intrusion into man's privacy,' he stated with distaste. 'There's something rather unpleasant about the idea of just anyone being able to invade your bath; I'm rather more choosy than that!'

Chloe clearly remembered from this morning the luxurious bathroom that adjoined his bedroom, the large round sunken bath that dominated the gold and cream room; yes, it was more than big enough for two people to share!

'Just a thought,' she dismissed.

'To what do I owe the honour of this call?' he prompted.

Your unthinking actions are threatening to destroy my father, my family, all over again! she wanted to scream at him.

But she didn't...

'I said I would ring,' she reminded him.

'And do you always do what you say you will?' Fergus commented throatily.

'I find it's usually best to, yes,' Chloe rejoined. 'How did the golf go?' she continued conversationally.

'Brice trounced me,' he answered with obvious disgust. 'What did you do to me last night, woman? I hardly had the strength to hit the wretched golf ball this afternoon!'

She hadn't done anything to him last night! At least, not in the way he meant. By the time she had driven him home, staggered up the stairs with him, got him undressed and into bed, he'd been out cold!

She laughed huskily. 'Poor Fergus,' she returned noncommittally.

She knew exactly what interpretation Fergus had put on finding her in his home, his bedroom, this morning. After her initial feelings of shocked dismay at the realisation, she had decided it might suit her purpose better if Fergus were to be a little unsure of himself where she was concerned. But, even so, she was not about to tell him an outright lie...

That would be reducing herself to the same level as the people who had already destroyed her father's career once. And almost destroyed their family too.

Eight years ago her father had been a prominent member of the government, in such a strong position politically that he would probably have become the next leader of his party, and so, in time, the next Prime Minister. But it had all come tumbling down around his ears when one of his aides, a woman, had committed suicide.

Susan Stirling had been aged in her mid-thirties, unmarried, not even in a long-term relationship—and she had been four months pregnant at the time of her death!

The newspapers had gone wild over the story, making a big issue as to who the father of her unborn child could possibly have been. Chloe's father had become the popular choice!

The scandal and speculation had rocked on for days, weeks—her father's official, and private, denials of the affair meaning nothing to the press.

It had been a nightmare; all the family hounded wherever they had gone, and Chloe's life at school had been made miserable as even she had been taunted with her father's so-called indiscretions. But her parents' marriage, thankfully, had survived the furore, her mother's trust in her husband unshakeable. And neither Penny nor Chloe had ever doubted their father's honesty for a moment.

But, finally, the Prime Minister of the time, with another election coming up some time during the following year, had been unwilling to let his government be shaken by such a public scandal, and had regretfully had to ask for her father's resignation.

Her father's place in his constituency had fared no better when the general election had taken place eight months later, her father losing his seat too as his opponent had used the unsolved scandal to his advantage.

Eight years her father had been in the political wilderness. Eight years!

And now, on the very eve of his attempt to restore his career, his campaign for re-election next year already underway, he was being threatened from a completely different source.

Whether he knew it or not, whether he cared or not, that source was Fergus McCloud!

And if it were humanly possible, Chloe intended stopping him!

CHAPTER THREE

'CHLOE…?' Fergus finally prompted when she hadn't responded to the question he had asked her several moments ago. Surely it didn't take this much thought to know whether or not she wanted to have dinner with him! After all, she had been the one to telephone him.

Which was something he wanted to discuss with her over the dinner he had just suggested they have together later this week…

'I'm sorry, Fergus.' She seemed to snap out of some sort of a daze. 'What did you say?'

Maybe she was just tired, too? After all, she couldn't have had much sleep last night, either!

'I asked if you would like to have dinner with me on Friday evening?' Much as Fergus would like to have seen her before then—if only to ask her several pertinent questions!—he had his mother staying in town for the rest of the week, plus he assumed that Chloe probably worked during the week, and the start of

50

the weekend would be more convenient for her, too.

'I would love to. Thank you,' she accepted warmly. 'Where shall we go?'

'Bernardo's?' It was the fashionable restaurant of the moment, the place where anyone who was anyone went to be 'seen'. While Fergus wasn't particularly into such things himself, he thought Chloe was probably still young enough to be.

Not that he had any idea exactly how old she was, but she looked to be in her early twenties. A bit young for him really—but he obviously hadn't seemed to mind that too much last night!

'Could we make it somewhere less... showbiz?' The grimace could be heard in her voice.

'Chloe Fox, you just went up several notches in my estimation!' he announced with satisfaction. 'I hate all that posing too,' he explained ruefully.

'Then why suggest we go there?' She sounded puzzled.

'I thought you might like it,' he answered honestly.

'Thanks—but no, thanks. We could always go to Chef Simon,' she suggested lightly.

'No!' came Fergus's immediate vehement response.

Although he, Logan and Brice had always been close, Fergus preferred to keep the rest of his family very firmly at bay. His Aunt Meg had recently married Daniel Simon, the owner of Chef Simon, and yesterday Logan had married Daniel's daughter, Darcy; the last thing Fergus wanted was to turn up at the restaurant with Chloe and find himself at the centre of family speculation about his own private life!

'Okay,' Chloe didn't question the reason for his protest. 'How about we go to Xander's instead? It's—'

'I know where it is, Chloe,' he interrupted, knowing exactly where the intimately exclusive restaurant was.

He just wasn't absolutely sure he liked the way this young lady kept overriding him and taking charge of things! Domineering women were not his favourite thing. He had his mother as a prime example of how destructive they could be. His father had only been able to take it for ten years before walking out on them both!

'Unless you have somewhere else quiet you would rather go?' Chloe suggested, redeeming herself slightly in Fergus's eyes.

But only slightly. Fergus accepted that she was the most exquisitely beautiful creature he had ever seen in his life, that they had spent the night together—obviously!—but that did not mean he altogether trusted her. She knew too much about him for him to feel confident enough to do that.

'No, Xander's is fine,' he confirmed evenly. 'I'll book a table for eight-thirty, if that's okay?' He was determined to choose the time, if not the place!

'Fine,' she agreed. 'I'll see you on Friday.'

'Er—Chloe?' He stopped her as he sensed she was about to ring off. 'It's customary where I come from for a man to call and collect his date for the evening,' he explained dryly.

'I thought it might be better if we went in my car. Just in case,' she added teasingly. 'I actually don't drink alcohol, you see.'

'Neither do I, to excess. Normally,' Fergus instantly defended; it was impossible to ignore the reference to his inebriated condition of last night, even if the remark had been made jokingly.

'You explained you were depressed about your cousin's wedding,' Chloe sympathised.

Fergus wasn't sure exactly what he had and hadn't said, and done, last night. And it wasn't a feeling he was comfortable with. He was usually so much in control, master of his own destiny, and all that.

'That was the champagne talking,' he dismissed harshly. 'I'm actually very pleased for Logan and Darcy.' And in retrospect he was. Yesterday's churlishness had faded. After all, he and his cousins couldn't have remained the Elusive Three for ever! 'I would also prefer to pick you up and drive you to the restaurant on Friday evening,' he said firmly.

'And I would prefer to meet you there,' she came back just as decisively.

Fergus grimaced his frustration with her stubbornness. Why didn't she want him to call at her home for her on Friday? Did she have something to hide? Someone? Just because she wasn't wearing a wedding ring didn't mean she wasn't in a permanent relationship; not everyone bothered to get married nowadays. Although, if that were the case, her partner must be a pretty weak character to have let her stay out all of last night. *He* certainly wouldn't be as understanding in the same circumstances!

'Please yourself,' he returned flatly. 'Now, if you don't mind, I'm rather cold and wish to return to my bath.'

He was also extremely irritated by this conversation. Something about Chloe Fox—and it wasn't just her seemingly domineering nature!—really annoyed him. They had spent the night together, gone to bed together, and yet he didn't feel that he knew her at all.

Well, on Friday evening he intended changing all that!

At least, he would have done—but Chloe had yet to turn up!

By eight-forty-five, he had been sitting in the restaurant for almost fifteen minutes, and there was still no sign of her. He was starting to feel decidedly uncomfortable!

The secluded corner table was set for two people, so it was obvious he was waiting for someone to join him, and he was starting to receive sympathetic looks from the other diners. When—*if*—Chloe ever did turn up, he was not going to be in the best of moods.

Besides which, he had ordered a bottle of wine while he waited for her, and he knew—to his consternation!—that he had already drunk two glasses of it in his increasing agitation. On an empty stomach too.

But he had been working hard today, and it wasn't unusual, when he worked, that he forgot to eat. Despite Maud's efforts to make sure that he was fed!

In fact, apart from spending some time with his mother before she returned to Scotland following the wedding, he had been working hard on research for his next book all week. It had been a way of diverting his attention while he'd waited for Friday evening to arrive!

Because, hard as he had tried, he hadn't been able to find out a single thing about Chloe Fox!

A few discreet enquiries to his friends and acquaintances hadn't turned up a single person who had ever heard of Chloe Fox. Directory Enquiries had been unable to help him too, when he had no idea of her address; the telephone book was apparently full of Foxes!

It was almost as if Chloe had appeared from out of nowhere. And, apart from that telephone call to him late on Sunday evening, had disappeared as completely.

He—

Wherever Chloe had disappeared to all week, she had now very definitely reappeared!

And, once again, she took his breath away!

If he had thought her exquisitely beautiful on Saturday night and Sunday morning, that was nothing to the way she looked tonight. And Fergus knew he wasn't the only one to think so.

Xander's was a discreetly exclusive restaurant, well accustomed to the rich and the famous coming through its doors. But as Chloe Fox moved gracefully through its crowded midst, the other diners fell silent, stopped eating their delicious food, in order to turn and look at her admiringly.

Her dress was bright scarlet red, Chinese in style, with a small mandarin collar, the silk material fitted to the perfection of her body like a second skin, its above-knee length leaving bare a long expanse of shapely legs. Her hair wasn't loose tonight but pulled back and secured on the back of her head in a neat chignon, the severeness of the style revealing the full extent of her unusual beauty.

Her skin was as delicate as magnolia, liner giving those deep blue eyes a slightly slanted appearance, her lips painted the same scarlet as her dress. She was, undisputably, the most beautiful woman in the room.

Fergus couldn't help feeling a certain satisfaction in knowing she was to be his partner for the evening.

He stood up as she approached their table. 'You look wonderful,' he told her as he pulled her chair back for her to sit down, his senses at once assailed with the delicacy of the perfume she wore.

Fergus had no idea what the perfume was, but he did know that he would never be able to smell it again without thinking of this woman. For good or bad!

'Thank you, Fergus.' She reached up to kiss him lightly on the cheek before sitting down. 'Isn't this a wonderful restaurant?' She looked around them with obvious pleasure.

While Fergus could only look at her!

He was thirty-five years old, had known many beautiful women in those years, quite a lot of them on a very intimate level. But he had never known any woman before who possessed Chloe Fox's sensually mesmerising beauty.

'Sorry I'm a little late.' She smiled at him now, revealing those tiny, even white teeth he remembered from last weekend.

But he couldn't help feeling slightly irritated when she offered no explanation for her tardiness. After all, he had been sitting here for almost twenty minutes, feeling more and more of an idiot as those minutes had passed.

'Would you like a glass of wine?' he offered stiffly.

She smiled ruefully. 'I really don't drink,' she refused with a shake of her head, turning to ask the waiter for some mineral water. 'Have you had a good week?' she turned back to enquire of Fergus politely.

His irritation increased. Politeness was fine, in its place, but between Chloe and himself he found it implied a distance that just shouldn't be there after they had spent the night together last Saturday.

'Very good,' he confirmed tersely; he had covered a lot of research towards his next novel this week, should be ready to start writing very soon. 'How about you?'

'I've kept busy.' She shrugged.

'Doing what?'

'This and that,' she dismissed, those blue eyes dancing with mirth as she looked across at him beneath lowered lashes.

Fergus couldn't miss the fact that her mirth was at his expense! This little minx knew exactly what he was doing—and she was just as determined not to be in the least helpful!

Fergus drew in a harsh breath. 'Chloe—'

'I'm sorry, Fergus, I shouldn't tease you.' She laughed huskily, reaching out to touch his hand briefly in apology. 'I'm a fashion designer.'

At last, he knew something about her other than her name! Not much, admittedly, but it was a start.

'Did you design the dress you're wearing tonight?' he prompted interestedly.

'Of course,' she dismissed, smiling up at the waiter as he brought, and poured, her water.

Of course...

In that case, her designs were excellent; the dress looked wonderful on her, suited her slender delicacy perfectly.

'Who do you work for?' he asked lightly, feeling the ice was breaking between them at last. In the circumstances, it shouldn't have been there in the first place!

Chloe sipped her water before answering. 'Myself,' she replied. 'But what about you, are you—?'

'You mean you're a freelance designer?' Fergus cut determinedly over what he guessed was going to be a deliberate change of subject on Chloe's part. Away from herself!

'Not exactly,' she answered noncommittally. 'Shall we look at the menus?' she said with a smile. 'I'm absolutely starving!'

She *was* changing the subject, damn it. Although he couldn't argue with the necessity of choosing their food; he had gone past starving himself and was now onto ravenous!

But if Chloe thought by looking at the menus and choosing their food he was going to let go of the only thing he had actually found out about her so far, then she was mistaken!

Chloe studied him surreptitiously from behind the shield of her menu. He had hidden it well, but she knew he had been absolutely furious when she'd actually arrived here this evening.

Not surprising, really; she had been almost twenty minutes late. Deliberately so.

One thing she had learnt about Fergus McCloud in the last few weeks: a simpering sycophant was not going to hold his interest for more than two minutes!

He was a man who had avoided a serious relationship, let alone matrimony, for at least the last fifteen years. Any woman who wanted to hold this man's interest for more than a couple of dates would have to be unusual, to say the least.

Although Chloe wasn't sure, as she saw that tightness about his mouth, the angry glitter in those warm brown eyes, that she hadn't gone too far. The last thing she wanted to happen was for Fergus not to even like her!

Because, strangely enough, she could all too easily like him…

He was interesting. Intelligent. Fun. His good looks unmistakable. And there had been something boyishly attractive, endearingly so, about his protectiveness towards her when his cousin Brice had arrived at the house last Sunday morning and found them there together…

Under any other circumstances, she was sure she would like Fergus McCloud very much indeed.

Again it was 'under other circumstances'…

She put her menu down on the table, smiling across at Fergus as he looked across at her enquiringly. She was right; he had started to feel wary of her. And that wasn't the idea at all!

'Actually, Fergus, I have my own label, sell my clothes to several well-known couturier shops,' she told him brightly.

'Very exclusive,' he guessed.

'Very,' she confirmed.

'And very expensive?' he drawled.

She laughed again softly. 'Of course.'

He relaxed slightly, obviously having just been given the answer to several more questions that he had concerning her; how she afforded her sports car and how she was so obviously at ease in these surroundings, to name but two. However, Chloe easily sensed that there were a lot more questions Fergus wanted answers to than those…

'What's the label called?' he prompted casually, putting his own menu down to give her his full attention.

Her mouth quirked. 'Would you believe, "Foxy"?' Not much help there!

Fergus gave a rueful smile. 'I'd believe,' he acknowledged. 'How come you and I have never met before, Chloe Fox? That I have never even heard your name mentioned before?'

Because until a year ago she hadn't lived in London all year round, had been at boarding-school in the south of England for years, before going on to university, and then she had spent a year in Paris with one of the top designers there. And in the last year she had been too busy getting her business off the ground to feature too much on the social scene.

There was also the fact that she hadn't been a hundred-per-cent honest concerning her name.

She shrugged. 'Just bad luck, I suppose,' she answered.

Fergus grinned. 'Yours or mine?'

'Both, of course,' Chloe returned. 'It would be very rude of me to say anything else.'

'You don't like to be rude. And you always try to do what you say you will,' Fergus murmured thoughtfully.

This man was making an inventory on what he slowly learnt about her! Not a good development.

'You might also like to know that I like to be fed at least twice a day,' she went on. 'And as I only had time for a quick breakfast this morning, and no lunch...' she added pointedly.

'You would like to eat now.' Fergus nodded, signalling to the waiter that they were ready to order.

Chloe studied him while the waiter noted their choices. Fergus's good looks weren't in doubt. Nor were his wealth or charm. But she would do well to remember not to underestimate his intelligence; Fergus was more than capable of adding two and two together and coming up with the correct answer of four. Maybe not tonight. But it wouldn't take too much probing on his part to discover exactly who the designer 'Foxy' was.

Telling him about that had been a calculated risk, but one she had deemed necessary in the face of his wariness. She wanted to keep his interest, but she wasn't going to get anywhere with him at all if she made herself too mysterious. And she still had a long way to go with this man if she were to achieve her objective.

'So tell me,' she said conversationally as the two of them enjoyed their starters, melon and strawberries in Chloe's case, and *moules marinière* in Fergus's, 'why didn't you want us to eat at your uncle's restaurant this evening?'

Fergus seemed to almost choke over the mussel he had just spooned into his mouth, looking across at her frowningly.

Chloe eyed him speculatively. 'Sorry—was I mistaken?' But she knew she wasn't, knew Fergus had been horrified at her suggestion that the two of them meet at Chef Simon this evening.

'Not at all,' he replied slowly. 'And the answer is simple, Chloe; I wanted to get to know you without any family distractions.'

There was a word for smooth flattery like this—but Chloe was too ladylike to even think it!

'How nice,' she returned as insincerely.

'I thought so,' Fergus replied. 'I'm sure you'll agree, there's still a lot we don't know about each other?'

What he really meant was there was a lot he still didn't know about her! Although he was obviously hoping to change all that tonight. If

Chloe had anything to do with it, he was going to be out of luck!

She smiled across at him. 'What's the saying? ''Finding out is half the fun''?'

'Probably,' he acknowledged dryly, not looking in the least convinced of the sentiment. 'I—'

'Chloe! It is Chloe, isn't it...?' the voice added less certainly.

Chloe's air of flirtation immediately deserted her as she looked up and easily recognised the man who had stopped beside their table.

Peter Ambrose!

It wasn't surprising that, having initially believed he recognised her, on closer inspection he was less sure; she had been fifteen years old the last time he'd seen her!

She swallowed hard, deliberately not looking at Fergus now; a previous brief glance his way had told her that he was stunned at the identity of the other man.

Which wasn't surprising! Until three years ago Peter Ambrose had been the British Prime Minister. Even now, he was still the Leader of the Opposition. And he obviously knew Chloe well enough to call her by her first name!

This was something she couldn't possibly have allowed for when she had decided to lay siege to Fergus McCloud!

CHAPTER FOUR

FERGUS once again found himself asking, who *was* Chloe Fox?

She was beautiful, intelligent, had a slightly wicked sense of humour, he was learning, but who *was* she?

'Peter,' she was greeting the other man warmly now as the two shook hands. 'How lovely to see you. Are Jean and the children all well?'

Fergus shook his head dazedly. Chloe also went to fashionable nightclubs, drove an expensive sports car, was a fashion designer with her own label—and she was on first-name terms with the former Prime Minister and his wife!

Peter Ambrose smiled down at her admiringly as he slowly released her hand. Too slowly, in Fergus's opinion!

'Jean is with me this evening.' The other man indicated a table across the room where his wife sat waiting for him. 'And the "chil-

dren'' are now aged twenty and twenty-two!'
he added wryly.

Chloe laughed softly. 'It's been a while,' she
acknowledged.

'Too long,' Peter Ambrose pressed warmly.
'I can't tell you how pleased we are to have
Paul back with us,' he continued more seri-
ously.

Paul? Fergus questioned inwardly. Who on
earth was Paul? He hated being in the dark like
this. It was even more galling when it was with
a woman with whom he had apparently been
on such intimate terms!

The question that was plaguing him the
most was just how intimate had her relationship with Peter Ambrose once been?

The other man, Fergus knew, was aged in
his mid-fifties, had been married to Jean for
over thirty of those years. But he was still an
attractive man, tall, slim, blond hair flecked
with grey; in fact, it was those relative good
looks that had helped him succeed in his en-
deavour to lead his political party.

And he and Chloe Fox obviously knew each
other very well!

Fergus felt the stirrings of the same unease
he had known last weekend when she'd been

so determined to join him; not just who was Chloe Fox—but *what* was she?

'I'm sorry, Fergus, I should have introduced the two of you.' Chloe turned belatedly to include him in their conversation. 'Peter, this is Fergus McCloud. Fergus, this is—'

'I know who he is, Chloe,' he rasped. 'Mr Ambrose.' He had stood up abruptly, briefly shaking the other man's hand.

'McCloud...?' Peter Ambrose repeated with a thoughtful expression. 'Why do I feel I should know that name...?'

Fergus's mouth twisted wryly. 'Probably because I have an appointment to come and see you on Wednesday,' he drawled.

'You do...?' The other man's thoughtful expression deepened. 'Of course you do.' His brow cleared. 'I remember now, you're the writer, aren't you?'

Fergus couldn't believe the coincidence of having bumped into this man this evening. Not that it was his coincidence. It was Chloe whom the other man knew; Peter Ambrose obviously wouldn't have distinguished him from one of the waiters serving on the tables here!

But Fergus still found it strange, after weeks of waiting to see Peter Ambrose, that he had met the man so casually this evening. Because Chloe Fox, a woman who had forced her company on him last Saturday evening, obviously knew Ambrose well. Very well, indeed.

'I am,' he confirmed evenly.

Peter Ambrose nodded. 'I remember my secretary thought you seemed very mysterious concerning your reasons for wanting to talk to me…?'

There was nothing mysterious about it at all, it just wasn't something Fergus intended talking about with anyone but the major players. And Chloe, no matter what her friendship with this man was—or had once been—wasn't one of them.

'I'm sure we really shouldn't keep you from your wife any longer, Peter,' Chloe was the one to put in decisively, looking up at the two men with cool blue eyes.

Peter Ambrose continued to look at Fergus probingly for several long seconds before turning slowly to smile at Chloe once again. 'You're right,' he agreed. 'It's really been lovely to see you again, Chloe. Let's hope I see you again very soon, hmm?' he added gently.

'I hope so,' Chloe replied.

'I'll look forward to seeing you again on Wednesday, Mr McCloud.' Peter Ambrose gave an acknowledging inclination of his head in parting.

Fergus slowly sat back at the table, his gaze narrowed thoughtfully on Chloe. She was a mystery within an enigma, an enigma within a labyrinth of unanswered questions. As a writer he wanted to solve that mystery. As a man, he hadn't got the least idea how he was going to go about it!

He drew in a harsh breath. 'You move in some pretty exalted circles, Chloe,' he ventured speculatively.

She resumed eating her fruit, her outward demeanour one of cool calmness. Outward, because, despite how she might want to appear concerning the unexpected encounter with Peter Ambrose, Fergus was sure he could detect a slight tremble to her hands.

'Not so exalted; Peter is no longer Prime Minister,' she countered.

'Chloe—'

'I knew his two children rather better than I ever knew Peter or Jean,' Chloe concluded.

Those children who at twenty and twenty-two were no longer children? Somehow Fergus very much doubted that she was telling him the whole truth. Despite the fact that Chloe was breathtakingly lovely, that he found her physically arousing, that he had obviously already spent the night with her, he had no use in his life for lies and deception.

Chloe looked across at him, her gaze unblinkingly compelling. 'You don't believe me, do you?' It was a statement rather than a question.

Fergus was momentarily taken aback by the directness of her attack 'I don't know what to believe,' he finally answered truthfully.

She put her cutlery back on her plate, her food still only half eaten as she looked at him coldly. 'Am I mistaken, or do you have the mistaken idea I've had an affair with Peter Ambrose?'

Fergus winced. Put into words like that, it sounded slightly ludicrous. And yet—because he didn't quite believe her explanation about knowing Ambrose's children—if she hadn't been involved with the other man, how on earth did she know him? Besides, it was noticeable that Jean Ambrose hadn't shared her husband's eagerness to come and say hello...

'You do.' Chloe sighed at his delay in responding. 'Fergus, I may be many things, but "the other woman" is not one of them. Do you believe that?' she pressed.

Strangely enough now he did. She had told him very little about herself, but suddenly he was sure that what she had just told him was the truth. He just found his whole relationship with Chloe—whatever it was!—totally beyond his control. And he wasn't comfortable with that. In the past he had always been the one to call the shots; Chloe, for all she was still extremely young, simply wouldn't allow him to do that.

'I believe you,' he sighed heavily. 'But there's something you aren't telling me, Chloe—'

'There's lots of things I'm not telling you, Fergus,' she admitted with a smile, her tension easing at his assurances. 'I'm sure you have absolutely no interest in hearing how cute my mother thought I was as a baby, what a little brat I was when I first went away to boarding-school, how studious I was at university, what a great time I had in Paris during the year following that. Wouldn't it be terribly boring if we already knew everything about each other?' she reasoned.

Well, of course it would, but that wasn't the point—

If he persisted with this, he would lose her! Fergus knew it as clearly as if she had said the words out loud...

'Apparently my mother thought I was cute as a baby too,' he returned. 'And the three of us, my two cousins and myself, were the bane of my grandfather's estate manager's life when we were growing up in Scotland. I didn't study quite so diligently at university as you apparently did, but I did okay anyway. I enjoyed my years as a lawyer, and I enjoy writing even more. But you're right, we don't need to know everything about each other by the second date.'

'Officially this is our first date,' Chloe corrected dryly.

And it had almost ended with Chloe getting up and walking out on him!

He had sensed it a few minutes ago, knew that she was ready to take flight if he persisted in not believing her. And he had suddenly known that, whoever she was, whatever she was, he didn't want her to go. Chloe Fox intrigued him, bewitched him, and he wasn't going to let her go out of his life until he had unravelled at least some of her mystery.

Chloe watched the expressions as they flitted rapidly across Fergus McCloud's face, sure that he had no idea just how much of his thoughts he was giving away.

It wasn't that he didn't believe her—he just didn't trust her!

Though she couldn't blame him for that, knew he was unsettled by the strangeness of their relationship anyway, that he had been totally thrown when Peter Ambrose had recognised her and come over to their table to talk to her.

That was nothing to the panic she had felt on recognising the other man!

Of all the things that could have happened, accidentally bumping into Peter Ambrose had to be the worst. However, on the other hand, without that accidental meeting she wouldn't have known of Fergus's appointment to see Peter on Wednesday…

Peter would be puzzled as to Fergus's reasons for wanting to see him; perhaps he believed, if he had given it any thought at all, that it was something to do with his political campaign to return his party to power in the general election next year. But Chloe had no such illusions.

She also knew, from listening to the two men, that her time was running out!

'Are you thinking of making a shift into politics next, Fergus?' she asked interestedly as their plates were cleared prior to the main course being served.

He laughed softly, shaking his head. 'Certainly not,' he replied vehemently. 'I like my privacy too much to even contemplate it.'

'But surely there's a certain amount of publicity involved in being an author?'

'Not enough to worry about,' Fergus assured her with satisfaction. 'Besides, do you think my personal life would stand up to the sort of intense public scrutiny that follows every politician?'

She raised dark brows. 'I don't know—would it?'

'No.' Fergus chuckled again. 'I've never been married, so no doubt the press would assume I have to be gay. And when they discover that isn't right, they would then commence speculating about my future marriage to every woman I even look at.' He shook his head again. 'I don't think so, thanks.'

Fergus painted a fairly awful picture for anyone entering public life. But, as Chloe knew all too well, it was also a correct one!

She had been pretty much protected from all of that by her parents during her childhood, but nevertheless she had known of the battering their own private life took on a day-to-day level. It had taken on horrific proportions after the scandal had hit the headlines eight years ago.

Chloe shrugged. 'Sorry. I just assumed, with the meeting you have with Peter Ambrose next week…?'

'Research,' Fergus replied, before sitting back so that their main course could be served.

The interruption couldn't have come at a worse time as far as Chloe was concerned. They were actually approaching the subject she was really interested in now—and their food had to arrive!

She was impatient for the waiter to leave, refusing vegetables or salad with her grilled salmon, although she had to sit by while Fergus was served a little from each of the four vegetable dishes to accompany his rare fillet steak.

'I'm hungry too,' he excused, once they had been left to enjoy their meal.

'You were telling me that you're research-ing a new book…?' Chloe tried again, picking uninterestedly at the salmon, her appetite hav-ing completely deserted her since Peter Ambrose had spoken to them.

Fergus leisurely finished chewing and swal-lowing a mouthful of steak before answering her. 'I don't believe I said it was for a book,' he replied guardedly.

Chloe gave him a frowning look, knowing he was being deliberately evasive. What else would he, an author, be doing research on if not a book…? Besides, she knew exactly what story he was researching!

'Just say if it's a subject you would prefer not to talk about,' she said lightly.

'It's a subject I would prefer not to talk about,' he repeated evenly. 'I don't mean to be rude, Chloe—'

'You're not making a good job of it, then,' she cut in teasingly, inwardly furious with her-self for giving him such an opening for a cop-out, but in truth, she hadn't really thought he would take it! He must be one of the few men she had ever met who didn't enjoy talking about himself!

Fergus sighed. 'Writing, I've found, is a very strange profession. Well, for me it is.' He grimaced. 'I've discovered from experience, that in the interest of keeping the story fresh and alive for me it's best if I never discuss my current work with anyone. Except my agent, of course.' He smiled. 'And even he only gets the barest outline of the plot so that he can sell the idea to the publisher!'

She was already well aware of that!

'Think of it in terms of your most recent designs, Chloe,' he continued slowly. 'I'm sure you don't share those with anyone else, either!'

'That's only because someone might steal the idea— You don't think that I would steal the plot for your book, do you, Fergus?' she exclaimed. 'I can assure you, I wouldn't have the least idea how to go about even starting to write a book!'

'Do you think it's true that everyone has at least one book inside them waiting to come out, given the right circumstances?' he asked.

She *thought* he was changing the subject—damn him. 'I just told you, I wouldn't even know how to start. That's why I'm so interested in the fact that you do,' she added huskily. 'One thing I do know, Fergus; your next book obviously has a political angle.'

'Maybe,' he returned evasively. 'Tell me, do you have brothers and sisters, Chloe?'

'An older sister,' she confirmed frustratedly; this was like getting blood out of a stone! 'You?' But she already knew that he didn't, had discovered that much about him at least.

'No,' he also confirmed. 'How about your parents? Are they both still alive?'

'I would hope so—they're only in their fifties, Fergus!' she rebuked, her parents, her father in particular, not a subject she wished to discuss with this man. Whatever information Fergus managed to find out about her father certainly would not come from her! 'How about yours?'

'Divorced. But both still alive,' he provided economically, suddenly fixing a compelling brown gaze on her. 'Tell me, Chloe, why are you so guarded about your own private life?'

Inwardly, she stiffened defensively at this sudden breach of good manners. Outwardly, she remained unshaken. She hoped. 'I wasn't aware that I was,' she answered levelly.

Fergus nodded. 'You know, Chloe, I have the distinct impression you're trying to hide something.' He eyed her humorously, but there was a steely edge to his tone.

Chloe forced herself to remain calm, meeting his steady gaze unflinchingly. 'Such as?' she prompted mockingly.

He shrugged. 'Maybe you're married? Or engaged? Or living with someone? Or maybe you're just an axe-murderess in search of a new victim?' he amended mischievously.

But Chloe wasn't fooled for a moment. That last remark had only been added for effect—it was the first three questions he was really interested in having an answer to. Did he really think she would be here with him now if any of those were true...?

'You guessed it—I'm an axe-murderess!' she replied unhelpfully.

Fergus didn't return her smile; instead he looked at her darkly. 'I'm not sure this relationship is going anywhere, Chloe,' he stated softly.

He was right, it wasn't. Not in the direction he wanted, anyway.

'I thought that was the way you liked it?' she returned abruptly.

'It is,' he responded slowly. 'But I find it strange, considering the two of us spent the night together last Saturday, that we don't seem to be making too much progress. In fact, we're behaving as if we're complete strangers to each other.'

He sounded genuinely regretful about that, and Chloe knew that she was the one to blame for that. She was the reason they weren't as relaxed and comfortable with each other as they should be. But how could she possibly be either of those things with Fergus when she knew he intended wreaking havoc in her father's life?

Because she knew exactly what Fergus's current book was going to be about, knew that he intended using the scandal that had wrecked her father's career eight years ago as the main focus of that story.

And the hardback of that book was scheduled to reach the bookshops only weeks prior to her father's bid for re-election!

CHAPTER FIVE

'EXCUSE the pun, Fergus,' Chloe said brightly, 'but you aren't exactly an open book yourself!'

He knew that. He had never been particularly close to any of the women he had been involved with over the years, let alone fallen in love with any of them. He preferred to keep his inner self to himself, never allowed any of his relationships to become too important in his life. In fact, he had been accused, more than once, of being distant and aloof. But he had never before encountered those very same traits in a woman. And a very young woman, at that.

'Touché,' he allowed. 'Do you think two clams like us are ever going to get to know each other?'

She smiled. 'As I've already said, we might have fun trying.'

They might. Fergus just wished that he could remember their being together last Saturday. It might help if he could remember how Chloe had felt in his arms, how her nakedness had felt next to his. Was she a silent lover, or did she give voice to her pleasure? He presumed he *had* given her pleasure; after all, she had been willing to see him again!

Suddenly he knew he had had enough of sitting in this restaurant, of the two of them trying to make polite conversation. He wanted to know Chloe. In the only way it seemed she would let him know her.

'Have you had enough of that?' He indicated the salmon on her plate she had been playing with, but not eating, the last ten minutes or so.

She looked startled. 'Yes...?'

'So have I.' He threw his napkin on the table-top, signalling the waiter to bring him the bill. 'Let's get out of here, hmm?' he prompted impatiently, standing up to move round the table and pull back her chair for her.

Chloe looked confused as she stood up too. 'But I thought you were hungry...?'

'I am.' He grinned down at her wolfishly, knowing his meaning wasn't lost on Chloe as colour suddenly highlighted her cheeks, giving darkness and depth to those beautiful blue eyes. Good; at least she hadn't become so cynical she couldn't still blush!

He still had no idea how old she was, but he would guess only twenty-three, or -four, at the most. But there was a reserve in her eyes, a wariness in her behaviour, that seemed to imply someone had once hurt her very badly. It was a reserve Fergus wanted to completely erase, if only for the time she was in his arms.

She seemed slightly dazed as he paid the bill, giving Peter and Jean Ambrose a brief wave goodbye before Fergus hustled her out the door.

Fergus had deliberately come by taxi this evening, but Chloe's car was parked only a short distance away, and he folded his long length into the passenger seat once she had unlocked the doors.

'I'd love to know how you got me in here the other night,' he murmured ruefully; his head touched the roof, and his knees were almost under his chin.

'The seat was further back that night. You'll find the controls on the door,' Chloe told him distractedly as she started the engine before pulling the car out into the flow of traffic.

Meaning someone else had sat in this seat during the last week, Fergus realised as he readjusted the seat so that it was more comfortable for him. Someone obviously several inches shorter than him...

Male or female? Fergus found himself wondering—and not liking the idea that it could have been another man. Chloe might be doing everything in her power to prevent him from getting to know her too well, but he found he certainly didn't like the possibility of there being another man in her life!

'Where are we going?' Chloe asked, beside him.

'Your place or mine,' he answered abruptly, still slightly disturbed by the thought of Chloe with another man.

'Yours, then,' she rejoined instantly, taking the turning that would eventually lead to his home.

Reminding Fergus that he still had several things he wanted to ask Miss Chloe Fox; how she had known last weekend where he lived, for one, and how she had known his telephone number so she could ring him on Sunday, for two!

But at the moment he was more interested in the fact that she had once again chosen not to give anything away about where she lived...

He turned to look at her consideringly, abstractly admiring the economy of her movements as she controlled the powerful car. 'Do you actually live in London?'

'Of course,' she confirmed in a puzzled voice.

'Alone?' he prompted softly.

Chloe turned to give him a brief glance before returning her attention to the road. 'No,' she finally answered.

Fergus felt himself tense at the admission. She didn't live alone! Then who—?

'I live with my parents, Fergus,' she informed him quietly. 'Hence the reason it wouldn't be a good idea for the two of us to go there. I take it you aren't into meeting parents?'

Too damned right, he wasn't! Especially the parents of a woman he had only met twice— and didn't really know at all!

'No,' he confirmed dryly. 'You're right, that could have posed a problem.'

She gave a half-smile. 'I thought so.'

Fergus gave her a considering look. 'You seem to know me rather well...?'

'Not at all, Fergus,' she dismissed laughingly. 'I think all men have a parent phobia!'

Unless they had serious intentions, yes. And Fergus had never had those, about any woman.

But he couldn't help wondering what Chloe's parents were like, if she still felt comfortable living with them. Surely that was unusual for a woman of her age; he remembered he hadn't been able to get out of his family home quick enough in order to set up his own bachelor apartment!

Obviously, Chloe came from a close family, then. Another fact about her he could add to the few he already had! Too few, in his opinion. But as she had already pointed out, at least they weren't bored with each other! Somehow Fergus was of the opinion that very few men would ever be bored in Chloe Fox's company!

'Who's Paul—? Careful!' Fergus instantly warned as Chloe veered the car sharply to the right. It would seem he had hit a sensitive nerve with his question...!

'Sorry,' she muttered, the car safely back on course now. 'I thought I saw a cat in the road.'

She had thought no such thing! Her face was slightly flushed, and those beautiful slender hands were tightly gripping the steering wheel; his question about the man Paul had completely unnerved her.

And she had neatly avoided answering it...

'I'm sorry, Fergus,' she said suddenly. 'But I seem to have developed a bit of a headache.'

And he had thought women saved that excuse for when they were married! He really had struck a sensitive nerve...

'Poor Chloe,' he sympathised. 'I'll get you something for it as soon as we get to the house.'

'I think, if you don't mind, that I would rather just call it a night and go home.' She grimaced.

Yes, he did mind! He still knew virtually nothing about this woman, had thought that once they were alone at his home that he would at least be able to hold her, to kiss her. Her decision to end the evening had put paid to that idea.

'Come in and have a cup of coffee first,' he encouraged as she stopped the car in the driveway.

'I really don't think—'

'I don't like the idea of you continuing to drive while you still have a headache,' he interrupted firmly, his gaze compelling. 'It's only a cup of coffee, Chloe,' he derided as she still looked uncertain.

'Okay,' she sighed, switching off the engine. 'Just a coffee.'

Fergus was frowning as he let the two of them into the house.

Unless he was very much mistaken, Chloe was fighting shy of any intimacy occurring between the two of them. Which, considering they had gone to bed together last weekend, was very strange...

Unless she had just decided, on closer acquaintance, that she wasn't attracted to him after all?

Whereas he, in complete contrast, had found that, on closer acquaintance, he wanted and desired Chloe Fox very much!

How on earth had she got herself into this situation? More to the point, how did she get herself out of it?

She had been completely stunned when Fergus had decided to leave the restaurant so precipitously, so stunned she hadn't been able to come up with a reason for them to have stayed, it must have been obvious to him that she'd no longer been eating her meal!

As for that question about Paul once they'd been in the car...!

Going back to Fergus's home with him had not been in her plans for the evening. She had intended saying goodnight to him after they'd left the restaurant. Although, she had realised once they'd been outside, ten-thirty had probably been a little early for that!

'Come through to the kitchen,' Fergus invited now. 'It's okay, Chloe,' he encouraged as she hung back reluctantly. 'My housekeeper will already have retired to her own rooms for the evening.'

If he meant to reassure her, he had failed miserably! She would have found it much more comforting to know that there was someone else around. Because it was one thing to act, for Fergus's benefit, as if they had spent the night together last Saturday, something else completely for him to expect that to actually happen again tonight!

She had been involved in relationships in the past, had even thought of marrying one of the men she'd met in Paris last year, but none of those relationships had ever gone beyond what she was comfortable with. She simply wasn't the type who could leap in and out of bed with a succession of men.

But Fergus believed they had already been to bed together once, and he would surely expect for it to happen again tonight...?

She should never have started this; it had been an act of madness on her part. Or desperation!

By the time Fergus had removed the jacket to his dark suit and had thrown it over the back of one of the kitchen chairs, moved economically around the kitchen preparing a pot of coffee, Chloe's headache was no longer a figment of her imagination!

'Here.' Fergus handed her two pills to go with the cup of coffee he had placed in front of her on the kitchen table.

He was being very kind and considerate, Chloe decided. Two of the qualities she had wanted to know he possessed. But did he have the third one; was he willing to make a personal sacrifice for someone else's benefit?

'I must say you do look rather pale.' He frowned down at her now. 'Let's go through to the sitting-room, I can switch the fire on in there and warm you up a little.'

She didn't want warming up, Chloe muttered to herself as she followed him out of the kitchen—she wanted to get out of here!

Preferably before—long before!—Fergus could discover that they hadn't made love together last Saturday.

It was a very male sitting-room, all golds and browns, the furniture sturdy, no feminine touches to soften its austerity. But, for all that, the room had the warmth of its owner. Which was added to considerably when Fergus turned on the promised fire, the flames almost looking real as they flickered through the artificial logs.

'That's better,' he said with satisfaction before coming to sit next to her on the sofa.

Bad choice, Chloe instantly realised, but the sofa had been the closest seat to the heat from the fire. She really wasn't very good at this. She couldn't help wondering what Fergus would have to say if he knew just how inexperienced she was!

She was very aware of him sitting close beside her, could feel the warmth emanating from his body, smell the slight tanginess of his aftershave. He really was a most attractive man, she acknowledged achingly as she looked at him beneath lowered lashes.

He turned to look at her, one hand moving up to smooth the wispy tendrils of hair at her temples. 'Feeling any better?' he prompted huskily.

She felt a sight worse with him close to her like this! Her legs were shaking, her hands were trembling as she still held her cup of coffee, and she couldn't seem to breathe properly, either.

She swallowed hard. 'Not really,' she replied, hoping he couldn't feel how nervous she was.

Fergus frowned some more. 'Perhaps you would feel better if you let this down.' He reached round to the neat chignon of her hair, deftly removing the four clips that kept it in place.

Her hair at once cascaded down in a curtain of midnight, and Fergus's fingers threaded through its silkiness as he helped release it about her shoulders, all the time his gaze locked darkly with hers.

Chloe's scalp tingled—but not from having her hair released. It was the touch of Fergus's hands, the desire so apparent in his mesmerising gaze, that gave her that thrill of sensation.

Oh…!

'You've done that before,' she attempted to tease.

He shook his head. 'Not that I can remember. But then, when I'm around you, I seem to have a problem even remembering my name!'

So did she. Or, at least, the parts of her name she had given him...

She moistened suddenly dry lips. 'Fergus—'

'That's it,' he confirmed lightly. 'My name is Fergus. And you're Chloe. Beautiful, sexy, desirable Chloe,' he murmured softly before his head lowered and his lips gently took possession of hers.

Chloe's whole body seemed to turn to liquid fire at the first touch of those lips, feeling as if she were melting, being consumed. She had never felt anything like this in her life before!

Fergus sipped from her mouth, tasted, his hands once again in her hair as he held her face up to his kiss, his tongue now moving searchingly over the sensitivity of her lips.

Chloe groaned low in her throat as she capitulated to that sensuality, instinctively reaching up to prolong the pleasure of those burning kisses—and instantly gasped as she felt burning of a completely different kind!

'What the—?' Fergus rasped as he hurriedly shifted away from her to look down dazedly to where Chloe had just tipped coffee over the two of them.

She had completely forgotten she'd still held the half-full coffee-cup in her hand as she'd reached up to touch Fergus!

'I'm so sorry,' she groaned awkwardly, relieved to feel that the coffee was rapidly cooling as it soaked through her dress—and Fergus's trousers.

'Well, that certainly put a dampener on things—literally.' Fergus grimaced as he gently took the cup and saucer from her lap to place them on the table behind them. 'I'll go and get a towel.' He stood up to quickly leave the room.

Chloe closed her eyes briefly once she was alone, leaning her head back against the sofa. She felt utterly, completely, stupid! What sort of moron forgot they were holding a cup of coffee in their hand? More to the point, what sort of moron did *Fergus* think forgot they had a cup of coffee in their hand?

'Here we are.' Fergus arrived back with the towel and, much to Chloe's embarrassment, proceeded to mop the coffee from her dress, the material now clinging to her damply.

Could this get any worse? she asked herself.

'Your dress is ruined, I'm afraid.' Fergus sat back to survey the wet silk when he had dried it as best he could. 'You'll have to take it off,' he added decisively.

It *could* get worse! It just had…!

Chloe hesitated before answering. 'It will soon dry—'

'Don't be ridiculous,' Fergus rejoined easily, standing up to reach out a hand to pull her to her feet. 'You need to slip out of that dress and into a hot shower.'

She didn't intend slipping out of anything— or into anything either, for that matter!

'There's really no need,' she assured him as she stood up. 'It's time I was leaving anyway.'

Fergus looked at her with narrowed eyes. 'I thought you were staying here tonight…?'

She was well aware of what he had thought—it just wasn't going to happen! 'I really do have a headache, Fergus,' she told him decidedly, deliberately not meeting that piercing gaze as she knew he continued to look at her.

And look at her…

He was obviously debating whether or not there were some way he could still persuade her to stay. He was wasting his time!

'Fine,' he finally rasped at her deliberately closed expression. 'I'll walk you to your car, then,' he offered with sharp dismissal.

Chloe didn't need to look at him to know that he was furiously angry. A cold, controlled anger. All the more unnerving because of that.

'Thank you,' she accepted huskily, walking through to the kitchen to collect her bag and keys. 'Perhaps we could have lunch together one day next week?' she suggested as the two of them walked to the door, Fergus a brooding presence behind her.

She had deliberately not mentioned the two of them meet over the weekend. Lunch, during the week, she had decided, with the excuse of returning to work to fall back on, would be infinitely safer than having dinner with him again; she doubted Fergus would expect her to jump into bed with him in the middle of the day!

'Perhaps,' he echoed noncommittally as he stood beside her open car door, Chloe already inside sitting behind the wheel.

But, from the tone of his voice, it wasn't very likely, Chloe realised heavily.

Maybe she should have stayed after all...? Maybe she could still have salvaged the evening, somehow brought the conversation round to the subject of Fergus's next book…?

Although, she had to admit, Fergus didn't look in the mood this evening to be told she had only wanted to know him at all in order to be able to gauge his response to being asked not to write his next book based on the scandal that had resulted in her father's resignation from government eight years ago! But, nevertheless, with the knowledge of Fergus's appointment with Peter Ambrose on Wednesday, Chloe knew she didn't have a lot of time left before the whole thing probably became public, anyway…

'I'll call you, shall I?' she prompted expectantly.

Fergus looked down at her, his expression readable in the light streaming from the open door behind him; his mouth was a thin, angry line, his eyes enigmatically hooded.

'I realise that until now you may have thought otherwise, Chloe—but I really prefer to do my own calling,' he finally bit out scathingly.

She looked up at him with a half-smile. 'You don't have my telephone number.'

'No,' he acknowledged shortly.

And he wasn't interested in knowing it, either, she realised with an inward wince. She really had annoyed him, hadn't she…?

But wasn't he being just a little arrogant too, in assuming that she would spend the night with him?

Arrogant or not, that was what he had thought—and he wasn't at all happy with the fact that she was leaving.

'Fine,' she echoed his own earlier terse dismissal, too shaken at the moment to argue the point. 'Thank you for dinner, Fergus,' she added softly. 'I enjoyed it.'

He raised dark brows over mocking brown eyes. 'You didn't eat it,' he pointed out.

She shrugged. 'I enjoyed what I ate.'

Fergus continued to look down at her, his presence in the open doorway meaning she couldn't actually close the door and drive away.

Why didn't he move? Exactly what was going on behind those enigmatic brown eyes?

Chloe knew she hadn't a hope of even guessing that if Fergus didn't want her to know! And he very definitely didn't!

'How does lunch, one o'clock on Tuesday, at Chef Simon, sound to you?' he finally said harshly.

And very reluctantly, Chloe realised ruefully. In spite of himself, Fergus was still intrigued by her.

In the circumstances, that was more than she could ever have hoped for!

But his suggestion of lunch on Tuesday—at Chef Simon, of all places!—meant she still had chance to talk to him before his appointment with Peter Ambrose on Wednesday. Probably her last chance!

It also, she realised more slowly, meant that Fergus would have the same opportunity to talk to *her* before his meeting with the other man. Fergus might be furious with her at the moment, but he wasn't so angry he hadn't been able to work that out…!

Because she knew that Fergus was puzzled by her friendship with the older man, had seen the unguarded questions in his eyes as he'd watched her in conversation with Peter.

On Tuesday, she decided with a nervously fluttering sensation in the pit of her stomach, all would have to be revealed; she couldn't leave it any longer than that without completely alienating Fergus.

And there was always the chance that she had already done that, anyway...!

CHAPTER SIX

'How is the delectable Chloe?'

Fergus didn't move a muscle as he sat in the window-seat of Brice's studio, and yet as he heard the question concerning Chloe a cold steeliness entered a gaze that had already been distantly preoccupied as he stared sightlessly out of the window.

'Or shouldn't I ask...?' Brice amended slowly as he looked over and obviously saw that steeliness.

Fergus drew in a sharply ragged breath, glancing over at his cousin as he stood putting the finishing touches to the portrait of Darcy he intended giving the newly married couple as a wedding present when they returned from their honeymoon.

Fergus had been here two hours now, sitting in this window-seat as Brice worked, unspeaking, totally absorbed in his own thoughts. And they had been far from pleasant!

'You shouldn't ask,' he confirmed bitterly, turning away to once again stare sightlessly out of the window that faced onto Brice's brightly sunlit garden.

Just what did Chloe think she was doing?

Damn it, he had asked himself that question over and over again the last twenty-four hours, and, with less than an hour to go before he was due to have lunch with Chloe, he was still no nearer finding an answer!

He refused to believe any longer that it could possibly be coincidence that she had spoken to him last Saturday. Or that she had gone to bed with him afterwards. So if it wasn't coincidence, what was it?

'Do you want to talk about it, Fergus?' Brice prompted concernedly as his cousin still watched him through narrowed lids.

Talk about what? What sense could Brice make of the last week that *he* hadn't been able to do?

Chloe had deliberately approached him that Saturday. She'd deliberately gone to bed with him. Despite the fact that he might have thought otherwise, she had lied to him. For what reason?

A word came to mind, but it was such an unpleasant one that Fergus found himself shying away from it.

Blackmail...

He winced as the word forced itself into his consciousness anyway.

'There,' Brice murmured with satisfaction as he stepped back from the canvas he had been working on. 'Come and look, Fergus,' he invited excitedly.

He stood up to stroll over and join Brice, glad of a diversion from his own thoughts. He was dressed completely in black; the black shirt and black denims perfectly reflected the darkness of his mood.

The painting was magnificent, of course, Brice having captured Darcy's unusual beauty perfectly: the deep red of her hair, the luminous grey eyes, the smile that reflected her inner warmth and caring. It was wonderful. There was no doubting Brice had a uniqueness of style that had made him the world-renowned artist he undoubtedly was.

'Logan is going to love it,' Fergus confirmed.

'I hope so,' Brice returned before turning to look consideringly at Fergus. 'Would I be wrong in assuming another of the Elusive Three is about to bite the dust?' he ventured.

Fergus flinched at the suggestion, his gaze hardening once again as he realised exactly what Brice was saying. 'You would be completely wrong in assuming any such thing!' he bit out with barely controlled fury. He wasn't falling in love with Chloe Fox—what he most wanted to do was strangle her!

Brice raised dark brows. 'I would?' he drawled sceptically. 'I don't believe I've ever seen you in this state over a woman before.'

Fergus's gaze flashed darkly. 'What state?'

His cousin shrugged. 'You've been here for hours now, you've barely spoken a word since you arrived, and if anything your mood became even blacker the moment I mentioned Chloe.'

Fergus's mouth twisted. 'And that implies I'm falling in love with her, does it?' he dismissed scathingly.

Brice grinned. 'It certainly implies she's got to you in a way I've never seen any other woman manage to do.'

Oh, Chloe had got to him, all right. But the more he thought about it, the more he was convinced it was by design rather than accident.

No doubt seeing him at the nightclub last Saturday had been pure luck; after all, he hadn't known he was going there himself until he'd actually got there. But what had followed had certainly been orchestrated by Chloe.

After days of puzzling over her hot-and-cold behaviour he had slowly been coming to the conclusion that it was because Chloe was a collector of famous notches on her bedpost. But now he realised differently. And the alternative explanation was no more palatable than the original one had been!

It was what he was going to do about it that was the real problem!

He sighed heavily, shaking his head. 'I have to go, Brice.' He glanced at his wrist-watch; twelve-forty-five. 'I'm having lunch with Chloe in half an hour.' He had been debating most of the morning whether or not he should meet Chloe at all, but now he had decided that fifteen minutes late should be long enough to deflate some of that self-confidence she seemed to have in abundance. It was high time Miss Chloe Fox was the one left guessing!

'Say hello from me.' His cousin nodded.

He gave a humourless smile. 'I'll do that.'

Brice gave him a considering look. 'She's very young, Fergus,' he said.

Old enough, as he knew only too well!

Fergus's gaze narrowed thoughtfully on his cousin. 'What's that supposed to mean?'

Brice shrugged. 'You're obviously angry with her about something.'

He shook his head disgustedly. 'Angry doesn't even begin to describe the way I feel at the moment!' he snapped.

'Exactly.' Brice nodded again.

He looked at his cousin, Brice raising mocking brows in response to that look.

'I'm hardly likely to strangle her at Chef Simon, Brice,' he drawled hardly. 'Far too public!'

Brice grinned ruefully at his attempt at humour. 'It would be a pity to mark that beautiful neck at all,' he opined.

Fergus smiled without humour. It came as no surprise to him that Brice was smitten with the way Chloe looked too; she really was the most incredibly beautiful young woman. The problem was, as he had found out, she was also manipulative and deceitful. Manipulative he could handle, it was her deceit he wasn't happy with.

'I'll bear your advice in mind, Brice,' he replied tersely, turning to leave.

'I liked her,' Brice offered softly from behind him.

Fergus's only response was a stiffening of his shoulders as he continued to walk out of the house. Damn it, he had liked Chloe too! Had. He wasn't completely sure how he felt about her any more!

God, she was so beautiful, was his first thought as he entered Chef Simon thirty minutes later and saw her seated at a table across the room.

Unaware of his critical gaze, she was staring pensively out of the window, obviously waiting for him to arrive, her chin resting on her raised hand, blue eyes troubled, those perfectly curving lips unsmiling as she thought herself unobserved.

She obviously believed he had stood her up!

Strangely, Fergus felt none of the satisfaction at her obvious uncertainty that he had expected to feel. A cold knot of anger seemed to have lodged itself in his chest, allowing room for no other emotion.

The fact that her face lit up with relieved pleasure as she turned and saw him approaching the table did nothing to alleviate that angry knot.

'Chloe,' he greeted tersely before bending to kiss her hard on the lips.

'Fergus...' she responded, lashes blinking over dazed blue eyes as she watched him warily as he sat down opposite her at the table, her tongue moving nervously across the lips he had just so arrogantly kissed.

'What's the matter, Chloe?' he taunted. 'Surely it's perfectly in order for me to kiss you hello? After all, we are lovers, aren't we?'

Her expression showed her confusion at his obvious aggression. Confusion! That was nothing to the emotions storming through him. He no longer wanted to strangle her, he decided; putting her over his knee and giving her a good hiding might afford him much more satisfaction!

Something was seriously wrong, Chloe realised warily.

Fergus was over fifteen minutes late for their luncheon date, and now that he had arrived he was like a cold, merciless stranger. Dressed all in black, his expression hard and unyielding, he looked like the devil himself!

How on earth could she even begin to talk to him about her father when he was in this mood?

'Fergus!' A tall attractive man whom Chloe easily recognised as Chef Simon himself came over to their table. 'I thought it must be you when I saw the booking.' He smiled warmly at Fergus. 'Good to see you again.' The two men shook hands as Fergus stood up politely.

'How's married life?' Fergus asked the other man conversationally.

Daniel Simon grinned. 'Wonderful!' he assured warmly before glancing enquiringly at Chloe.

The coldness in Fergus's eyes hit her like a blast of ice as he also turned to look at her, causing her to recoil involuntarily. He looked as if he hated her!

Admittedly he hadn't been too happy with her when they'd parted on Friday evening, obviously disappointed that she'd been leaving so suddenly, but he certainly hadn't hated her then. What could have happened in the intervening three days to have caused this change in him…?

Chloe felt a nervous fluttering in the pit of her stomach at the realisation that something *had* changed.

'Daniel, this is Chloe,' Fergus introduced economically. 'Chloe, my uncle, Daniel Simon,' he added less coldly.

'Pleased to meet you.' Daniel Simon shook her hand. 'I hope the two of you will excuse me; I have to get back to the kitchen. I hope you enjoy your meal,' he added hospitably.

Chloe gave the stony-faced Fergus a look beneath shadowy lashes as he resumed his seat opposite her; she had a distinct feeling neither of them were going to enjoy any part of their meal!

She had dressed with extra care herself to-day, wearing a tailored silk trouser suit the same colour blue as her eyes, her hair loose and silky down the length of her spine. But for all the notice Fergus had taken of the way she looked, she might just as well have worn a sack!

'What's wrong, Fergus?' she asked after several awkward moments of silence, neither of them making any move to look at the menus that lay on the table-top, either.

His eyes were dark as coal as he looked across at her. 'Wrong?' he echoed distantly. 'Why should anything be wrong?'

Chloe felt an apprehensive shiver down the length of her spine. Fergus had never been that easy to talk to, but he was like a stranger today, a cold, unapproachable stranger.

She swallowed hard. 'You seem—different, today…?' she tried again.

His mouth twisted humourlessly. 'Different from what?'

Chloe frowned. 'I'm not sure,' she admitted.

Fergus gave a dismissive shake of his head. 'I have no idea what you're talking about, Chloe. And I'm not sure you do, either,' he added insultingly before picking up the menu. 'Shall we order?' he prompted.

Chloe continued to look at him searchingly, not liking the challenge in those hard brown eyes as Fergus looked straight back at her.

She had known before she'd come here today that this was her last opportunity to talk to Fergus, that once he had seen and spoken to Peter Ambrose tomorrow he would probably know exactly who she was. But with Fergus in this mood, how did she even begin to approach the subject of her father?

'What do you want, Chloe?' Fergus suddenly bit out hardly.

She gave a guilty start at the abruptness of the question coming so soon on top of her troubled thoughts. 'I—I wasn't aware I wanted anything,' she finally answered him awkwardly.

His mouth twisted again. 'I was actually referring to your lunch,' he drawled mockingly, with a pointed look up at the hovering waiter.

'Oh!' Colour darkened her cheeks as she hastily looked down at the menu. 'I'll have gazpacho, followed by the monkfish,' she requested hollowly. 'With a green salad.' She closed the menu with a decisive snap.

'So...' Fergus turned to her once they were alone again '...have you been working this morning?'

Hardly; she had been too nervous about this lunch with Fergus to even begin to concentrate on her designs. Besides, she had the distinct impression Fergus wasn't really interested in what she had been doing this morning...

'Not really,' she responded lightly.

He raised dark brows. 'Did you do anything nice over the weekend?'

She shrugged, becoming more and more convinced that Fergus wasn't really interested in her answers to his polite questions. In fact, she had a strange feeling of foreboding, as if there were a sword hovering above her head!

'Not particularly.' She shrugged once more. 'How about you?' Two could play at this game!

Somehow, for reasons she was as yet unaware of, the tables had been turned; Fergus was no longer the one who was unsure of her, it was the other way around.

'I'm still working on the research for my next book,' he answered.

'The political thriller.' She nodded; at least the conversation was going in the direction she wanted it to. 'Have you started writing it yet?' she added casually, trying not to look too interested in his answer as she turned to break the bread roll on her plate.

'Not yet,' he said. 'I like to do all my research first. Be sure of all my facts.'

'It wouldn't do for someone to sue you for defamation of character,' she attempted to tease—and failed miserably. Her father couldn't sue; the puzzle of the identity of

Susan Stirling's lover, and the father of her unborn child, had never been solved.

'I'm a lawyer, Chloe; I know just how far I can go. Are you interested in politics?' Fergus prompted softly.

Chloe's breath caught in her throat. She had been brought up on a diet of politics for breakfast, lunch and tea; how could she not have an interest in them?

'You have your opening now, Chloe,' Fergus persisted. 'But do you have the guts to take it, I wonder?' he added with hard mockery.

She looked sharply across at him, feeling the colour draining from her cheeks as she once again met the hard challenge in those enigmatic brown eyes. Strange, when she had first met him she had thought his eyes were like warm chocolate; today they resembled brown pebbles of ice!

She swallowed hard. 'What do you mean?'

'I don't like guessing games, Chloe. I never have,' he told her coldly. 'And you're demolishing that bread roll into inedible crumbs,' he observed.

Chloe snatched her hand away as she saw she had indeed been shredding the bread to pieces. Without even realising she was doing it. So much for looking uninterested!

'I asked if you're interested in politics, Chloe,' Fergus repeated harshly.

'I—' She tried to speak, but her jaws seemed to be locked together!

He knew! She didn't know how he knew, but she was sure that he did...

Fergus leant over the table, his face only inches away from her own now. 'Come on, Chloe Fox-*Hamilton*, answer the question, damn you!' he bit out between gritted teeth.

Chloe Fox-Hamilton. Yes, he did know!

She moistened dry lips. 'Fergus—'

'I have no idea how you know anything about the plot for my next book,' he ground out evenly. 'Although, I can assure you, I do intend finding that out,' he added warningly. 'But one thing I do know, Miss Fox-*Hamilton*,' he grated insultingly. 'The fact that we've been out together a few times, that you've shared my bed, is not going to affect the writing of that book one iota. Do I make myself clear?' he finished with cold deliberation.

As crystal!

CHAPTER SEVEN

LAST Saturday night, dinner on Friday, all those things Chloe had known about him, to her they had only been a means to an end. Yes, going to bed with him had only been a means to an end!

Maybe in the case of the latter it was his hurt pride that made him feel so angry, but knowing the reason for it didn't lessen the emotion.

Fergus looked across the table at Chloe now with furiously glittering eyes. 'Tell me, Chloe—I'm curious to know—besides seducing me, exactly what was your plan of action?'

She looked startled. 'I didn't—'

'Oh, please.' He held up protesting hands. 'Being Paul Hamilton's daughter, you must have had some plan in mind.'

Her cheeks flushed angrily, eyes flashing deeply blue. 'Don't talk about my father in that derogatory way!'

Yes, he decided consideringly, he could see the likeness between father and daughter now, the same dark hair, the same deep blue eyes, a certain similarity in the facial structure.

Chloe was the daughter of the former Minister Paul Hamilton. That was how she knew Peter Ambrose. How Peter Ambrose knew her. Now that Fergus knew the truth of Chloe's identity, he wasn't sure he wouldn't have preferred his first assumption about their relationship to have been the correct one!

He had been eaten up with the knowledge of Chloe's true identity since learning of it yesterday, hadn't slept, hadn't eaten, going over and over in his mind the events of the last eleven days. And not once had those conclusions actually taken him to the point where he could believe Chloe even liked him, let alone anything else!

If he were honest, that was what really rankled about this situation. Because he liked—*had* liked—Chloe, too much for comfort!

He gave a deep sigh. 'What do you want from me, Chloe?' he asked wearily.

Tears glistened in the deep blue eyes as she looked at him. 'I want you to leave my father alone. Find another plot for your book. Hasn't he suffered enough?' she burst out, choking with emotion.

Fergus forced himself to remember just how deliberately Chloe had entered his life, hardening himself to those tears. 'Susan Stirling's family probably don't think so—'

'My father was not involved with Susan Stirling!' she defended fiercely.

He raised an eyebrow. 'The consensus of opinion seems to think otherwise—'

'I'm not interested in the consensus of opinion!' Chloe cut in, still emotional. 'My father loves my mother, is still *in* love with her,' she added with certainty.

Fergus grimaced. 'All children like to believe that of their own parents.'

Her eyes glittered with anger now instead of tears. 'How would *you* know? Your parents are divorced—I'm sorry!' She gasped, putting a regretful hand up to her mouth. 'I shouldn't have said that.'

'No—you shouldn't,' Fergus acknowledged in a dangerously soft voice. 'Look, Chloe,' he continued more gently. 'I understand that you love your father, and because of that love you believe in his innocence—'

'The admiration and love I feel for my father have nothing to do with it,' she declared determinedly. 'Well...obviously they have something to do with it,' she amended self-consciously at Fergus's derisive snort. 'But the truth of the matter is that he *is* innocent of any involvement with Susan Stirling!' She looked across at Fergus as if daring him to contradict her a second time.

Fergus looked back at her for several long seconds, compassion for her conviction warring inside him with the anger he personally felt towards her for her deliberate duplicity where he was concerned. Admiration, too, he admitted grudgingly, that she was willing to go to such lengths to protect her father.

'Eat your soup,' he finally said stiffly. 'Before it goes cold,' he added at an attempt at humour.

Chloe didn't look any more interested in eating her food than he did, picking up her spoon to stir the chilled soup disconsolately round in the bowl.

Finally she sniffed indelicately. 'I always thought that in this country a man was presumed innocent until proven guilty.' She muttered this gruffly, her head bent as she still stared down at her untouched soup.

'He is,' Fergus confirmed heavily.

Damn it, she *was* crying! He could see the trickle of tears now against the paleness of her cheeks.

She sniffed again. 'Are you aware that my father is going to stand for re-election next year?'

'I am now.'

Chloe did look up now, more, as yet unshed, tears brimming to spilling point against her lashes. 'How—?'

'Peter Ambrose had to bring our appointment forward to yesterday instead of Wednesday,' Fergus told her heavily.

He had felt as if the other man had hit him in the stomach with a sledgehammer when Peter Ambrose had unwittingly revealed that Chloe was Paul Hamilton's daughter, expressing surprise that Fergus and Chloe should seem so close considering Fergus was researching a book based on the scandal in her father's past. In fact, Fergus had been so stunned, he wasn't sure how he had conducted the rest of the interview!

He had been in an angry fury ever since. Everything that had puzzled him about Chloe had added up once he'd had that piece of information: Chloe's persistence last Saturday, the fact that she knew where he lived, his telephone number, even how he took his coffee, for goodness' sake.

Although how she knew about his book in the first place he had yet to find out...?

'Chloe, who told you I was writing this particular book?' he said slowly.

She turned away. 'Isn't it enough that I know?' she dismissed raggedly.

'No,' Fergus answered firmly. 'As yet only a few people, like my agent and the publisher, are aware of even the barest outline of the plot of my next book. And yet you seem to know about it too.' He frowned darkly.

She paused. 'I just know, okay?' she came back with uncharacteristic aggression.

No, it was not okay. Until he had spoken to Peter Ambrose yesterday, only a handful of people had been privileged to know that information, and none of them had been at liberty to discuss it with anyone else. Besides, he couldn't help but be aware that Chloe was deliberately not meeting his gaze...

'Do you really still intend writing the book?' She looked at him intently. 'Even now that you know my father is going to stand for re-election,' she explained impatiently as Fergus raised derisive brows.

His mouth tightened, knowing Chloe wasn't going to like his answer. His whole plot-line hinged on that scandal. Besides—and Chloe wasn't going to like this one little bit!—he was one of the people who did believe her father was guilty of what he was accused...

Besides, that wasn't really what Chloe was asking! 'Don't you mean, now that the two of us have slept together?' he drawled.

She gasped. 'We—I didn't—'

'I told you, Chloe, I don't like games,' he bit out coldly, looking across at her with cool cynicism. Did she really think that he would change his mind about writing the book just because she had been to bed with him? He shook his head. He didn't think Chloe had really given this much thought at all!

Her head was still bowed. 'I just wanted to talk to you.' Her words were barely audible now, her voice husky with emotion. 'Plead with you, if necessary, not to do this to my father,' she added shakily.

'Then why the hell didn't you just use the normal means for meeting someone?' he rasped hardly. 'Such as telephoning and asking for an appointment!'

She looked up at him with emotionally bruised eyes. 'And once I had told you my name was Hamilton, would you have agreed to see me?' she challenged disbelievingly.

No! Yes! Probably... Maybe, he finally conceded. After all, she was close enough to Paul Hamilton to—

What *was* he thinking? Chloe might have gone about this the wrong way, and he was furiously angry at being taken for a fool, but that didn't mean he had to compound the situation by behaving exactly as she had obviously imagined he would!

'Probably out of curiosity,' Chloe acknowledged as she seemed to read the emotions flitting across his face. 'But nothing else,' she concluded.

Fergus found that he didn't like having his reactions and feelings predicted for him in this way. No, he didn't like it at all.

'So you decided to meet me, giving me a not exactly accurate version of your name, manoeuvre me into a compromising situation, and—then what, Chloe?' he demanded scathingly. 'Blackmail? After all, I wouldn't come out of the affair looking too good if it became publicly known that I had actually had a relationship with the daughter of Paul Hamilton, now, would I?'

If anything Chloe's face had gone even paler, the darkness of her brows and lashes standing out starkly against the whiteness of her skin, her eyes deep blue pools of pained emotion.

Fergus felt himself melting inside, hating the fact that he was the one responsible for that pain.

No! He mustn't weaken. Chloe had deliberately manipulated this situation, and she hadn't given a damn about him as a person while she'd been doing it. If he weakened now he would find himself agreeing to anything she asked of him—including scrapping a book he had already done weeks of research on!

'Have you ever met my father?' she asked quietly.

His mouth tightened. 'Not yet.'

'But you intend to do so before you begin writing your book?' she persisted.

'Probably,' he conceded grudgingly. He had no intention of telling Chloe he had an appointment to see her father on Friday morning;

he was still angry enough with her to want her to squirm a little longer!

She nodded. 'Then I suppose I'll have to settle for that.'

Fergus's mouth twisted. 'The implication there being that once I've met him I'll know I'm wrong about him?' he taunted.

Her head went back proudly. 'Yes.'

Fergus shook his head again. 'I think you're being more than a little over-optimistic there, Chloe.'

'And *I* think we'll just have to wait and see,' she said stubbornly.

'You went too far in going to bed with me, Chloe,' he rasped harshly. 'Besides which,' he went on, 'as I'm sure you are all too well aware, I have absolutely no memory of the incident. So if you intend going to the newspapers with this, I—'

'You really do believe I was going to blackmail you?' Chloe gasped disbelievingly.

Fergus looked at her coolly. 'What else?'

Chloe was breathing deeply, two bright spots of angry colour on her cheeks now. 'For the record, Mr McCloud—'

'Whose record?' he cut in with mocking disdain.

'Anyone who cares to listen!' She had raised her voice now so that the people dining on the surrounding tables could hear what she was saying. 'For the record, Mr McCloud,' she repeated slowly and clearly, 'I did not share your bed last Saturday, I spent the night—the whole night!—sitting in your bedroom chair.'

Fergus didn't move, feeling as if he were glued to his seat, only his gaze flicking reluctantly around the room. But it was enough to show him they had the attention of all the other diners in the room now, even the *maître d'* and the waitresses stopping in their work to turn and look at them.

He winced. 'Chloe,' he began softly.

'I did not share your bed, Mr McCloud,' she continued with determination. 'And even if I had chosen to do so, you had drunk so much champagne you were totally incapable of my being able to accuse you of doing anything other than sleeping. Have I made myself clear enough?' she challenged scornfully.

More than clear, he would have said! 'I'm not sure the people in the kitchen heard you,' he said sardonically, as he knew himself the object of every gaze in the restaurant.

Chloe gave a scathingly pointed glance in the direction of the kitchen as she stood up, Daniel and a couple of his assistants having appeared in the open doorway. 'Obviously they did,' she snapped. 'If you'll excuse me…' She gave him a sharply dismissive nod before turning to walk across the room, her head held high.

God, she was magnificent, Fergus acknowledged admiringly as he watched her go. Absolutely magnificent. She looked like some exotic princess as she strode confidently through the room, her shoulders back proudly, her head held high, that gloriously long dark hair cascading down to her waist.

'Come through to the kitchen.' Daniel spoke gently at Fergus's side as the restaurant door closed behind Chloe, a soft buzz of conversation immediately starting to fill the room.

Fergus stood up, feeling almost disorientated, allowing the older man to take his arm and lead him into the aromatic warmth of the restaurant kitchen.

'What is it about my restaurant, and you Scottish cousins?' Daniel shook his head ruefully once the door had closed behind them. 'Still, let's look on the bright side,' he added with amused derision. 'At least Chloe didn't tip the bowl of gazpacho over your head before she left!'

Fergus wasn't so fazed by Chloe's dramatic departure that he didn't realise Daniel was referring to his daughter Darcy's relationship with Fergus's cousin Logan. Logan had seemed to spend most of that courtship removing one substance or another from himself, or his clothing, that Darcy had either thrown over him deliberately, or accidentally.

'We didn't go to bed together, Daniel,' he told the other man with vehemence.

The older man's mouth quirked. 'I think we can all safely assume that,' he confirmed dryly.

'Exactly,' Fergus murmured with satisfaction.

And the fact that they hadn't, that Chloe had announced it in the middle of a crowded restaurant, didn't dismay him as it should have done. In fact, he couldn't have felt happier!

What had she just done?

Chloe dropped thankfully into the back seat of the taxi she had just flagged down to take her home, having scrambled hastily inside as soon as it had stopped, sure she could still feel

Fergus's hot and angry breath on the back of her neck.

But a quick glance out of the window showed her that he hadn't followed her, after all. Not that she would have blamed him if he had; she had just announced in front of at least forty people that he had been incapable of making love to her the other Saturday night!

What on earth had possessed her to do such a thing?

The answer to that was simple enough, she acknowledged heavily. She had been goaded into it by Fergus's claim that she intended blackmailing him into silence with the fact that they had been to bed together.

She cringed just at the memory of all those shocked faces as she'd loudly announced that the two of them hadn't slept together at all.

Oh, she had made a mess of this. A complete and utter mess.

Instead of arousing Fergus's sympathy and understanding where her father was concerned, she had only succeeded in arousing his anger and scorn—towards her! Worst of all, Fergus seemed more determined than ever to go ahead and write his book.

And some time—in the very near future!—
she was going to have to break the news of
that to her parents. It wasn't something she
looked forward to at all!

Although there was no opportunity to do
that over the next few days. Her father and
mother were away visiting the constituency her
father intended contesting, and it was hardly
the sort of thing she could break to them during one of their brief nightly telephone con-
versations to check that she was all right!

When her parents returned on Thursday evening, they both looked so tired Chloe didn't
have the heart to even broach the subject. And
Friday was her sister's and David's wedding
anniversary, the five of them due to go out to
dinner to celebrate, so that was out too.
Hopefully some opportunity would present itself over the weekend.

Chloe knew she simply couldn't leave it any
longer than that; if Peter Ambrose hadn't spoken to her father yet, he very soon would do.
But it would be better coming from Chloe first.
If only so that she could explain her own acquaintance with Fergus!

Although quite how she went about doing
that she wasn't sure, either!

She had heard nothing from Fergus. Not that she had expected to after that fiasco in the restaurant, but, even so, she knew that where he was concerned no news was not good news!

Which was why, when she came downstairs on Friday morning, on her way out to buy a gift she could give to Penny and David that evening, she was totally stunned, after giving a cursory glance inside the small reception room off the main hallway, to see Fergus sitting in there!

She gasped, her cheeks paling as she hastily entered the room, pulling the door closed behind her. 'What are you doing here?' she snapped accusingly. As if she really needed to ask!

Fergus looked perfectly relaxed as he glanced up at her. 'Taking your advice, of course; meeting your father,' he said casually, lounged in one of the armchairs, formally dressed today in a dark suit and blue shirt with matching tie.

Her cheeks coloured bright red as she remembered the occasion when she had given that advice. What had Fergus done that day after she'd left the restaurant? Had he carried on eating his meal? Or had he decided it was time to leave too? Somehow she thought it would have been the latter!

She had dreaded the possibility of their next meeting, still cringed whenever she thought of her behaviour in the restaurant; but she certainly hadn't ever expected they would meet again at her parents' home.

'You're still going ahead with it, then,' she realised dully.

Fergus slowly stood up, his height instantly dominating the room, the intensity of his guarded expression giving lie to his previously relaxed pose. 'I'm here to meet your father,' he repeated unhelpfully.

But, then, why should he feel disposed to be helpful? The last time the two of them had met she had publicly embarrassed him!

'His assistant, David, has just gone to tell him I'm here,' Fergus elaborated.

'Fergus.' Chloe looked up at him with pleading eyes, reaching out to put a hand on the rigid hardness of his arm. 'Please don't let the animosity you must have towards me influence how you ultimately feel towards my father.'

Brown eyes narrowed as he looked down at her. 'Are you going out?' He looked pointedly at the jacket she had recently put on over her tee shirt and jeans.

'I was…' she confirmed slowly, not sure that she should do so now that Fergus was here to see her father. Besides, she hadn't missed the fact that Fergus hadn't answered her question… 'Why?' she prompted warily.

Fergus shrugged. 'No reason. I had just thought that perhaps the two of us could have lunch together once I've finished talking to your father.'

He had just thought—! 'I very much doubt that we will want to! Besides, do you really think that's a good idea—after last time?' she came back swiftly.

He gave a smile. 'I wouldn't advise you to try that dramatic exit a second time,' he drawled. 'Obviously there were no reporters present at Chef Simon on Tuesday, but you may not be so lucky next time,' he pointed out.

She had lived in dread, the last couple of days, of one of the gossip columns mentioning the incident at Chef Simon on Tuesday, but, as Fergus said, she had been lucky.

She drew in a ragged breath. 'I'm really sorry about Tuesday. I just—you—'

'Just leave it at the apology, hmm, Chloe,' he silenced softly, lifting a hand to gently stroke the creaminess of her cheek. 'As far as I can see, we were both out of order. And Daniel has assured me it did business no harm whatsoever; it seems most people lingered over coffee and liqueurs in order to talk about the incident!'

Chloe could believe that; it had been rather a spectacular show! 'I must say, you seem to be taking it rather well,' she said uncertainly.

He shrugged again. 'I think my reputation as a lover may have taken a bit of a knock, but what the hell? You—'

'Mr McCloud, I'm so sorry to have kept you—Chloe…?' Her father looked at her questioningly as, having entered the room to meet Fergus, he found Chloe in there talking with the other man. 'I didn't know the two of you knew each other…?' he added with light enquiry.

Chloe gave an awkward glance in Fergus's direction before turning back to her father. 'I—'

'Oh, Chloe and I are old friends,' Fergus put in firmly, calmly meeting the stunned look she turned on him. 'In fact I was just inviting her out to lunch,' he added.

Chloe was confused. Exactly what was Fergus up to? They most definitely were not old friends; nearly two weeks of acquaintance made them far from that! And if the positions were reversed, if Fergus had done to her what she'd done to him at the restaurant on Tuesday, she certainly wouldn't be inviting him out to lunch a second time!

She gave him a narrow-eyed look before beaming up at her father. 'Unfortunately I was having to refuse, because I really do have to get into town to do some shopping,' she explained gracefully.

'Then it looks as if it will have to be dinner instead,' Fergus accepted, unperturbed.

Angry colour—at his arrogance—flared in her cheeks.

'It would seem you're going to be unlucky for the second time today, Mr McCloud,' her father was the one to answer him laughingly. 'We have a family celebration this evening. My eldest daughter's twelfth wedding anniversary,' he explained at Fergus's questioning glance. 'Although I suppose there's no reason,' he continued thoughtfully, 'if you don't mind sharing my beautiful daughter with the rest of her family, why you can't join us. If you would care to?'

Chloe gasped her horror of the suggestion. But one glance at Fergus, at the mocking humour in his eyes as he easily met her horrified glance, and she knew he was going to accept the invitation!

How could he?

How *dared* he!

CHAPTER EIGHT

FERGUS had guessed, from her glaring look in his direction, that Chloe expected him to refuse the invitation. That, in itself, was enough to make him want to accept!

'I'll leave the two of you to discuss it,' Paul Hamilton told them tactfully as he sensed their indecision. He turned to smile at Fergus. 'Chloe will bring you through to my study when you've finished talking.'

Fergus watched with observing eyes as the older man left the room. Paul Hamilton looked exactly like the numerous photographs Fergus had of him. But those photographs hadn't been able to project the candidness of his gaze, or the warm pride in his voice as he talked of his beautiful daughter...

'You have to refuse,' that beautiful daughter was now telling Fergus in an angry hiss. 'You couldn't be so hypocritical as to accept!' she added disgustedly.

The high colour in her cheeks suited her, Fergus decided abstractly, adding to her beauty, and giving depth to the angry blue sparkle of her eyes.

He hadn't been sure whether or not he would see Chloe here today, but he had certainly hoped that he would. For one thing it had saved him the humiliation of telephoning her and having her refuse to take his call! And for another, he had just wanted to see her again...

She looked very young today in the casual denims and tee shirt, the sophisticated fashion designer nowhere in sight. In fact, she looked wonderful. But then, she always did...

'Don't be ridiculous, Chloe,' he answered her sternly. 'You already believe I'm hard and uncaring, so why not add hypocrite to that list?'

'Because—because you just can't!' she told him frustratedly, looking as if she would like to stamp her foot in protest, but considered it too unladylike.

Fergus held back a smile. 'Of course I can. Your father just invited me.' He held up his hands.

Chloe glared up at him. 'My father could regret that invitation, once the two of you have talked this morning!'

'He might,' Fergus agreed unconcernedly. 'But I'm sure he's too polite to withdraw the invitation once it has been accepted. And I do mean to accept.'

'I can't believe this!' Chloe turned away, walking over to stare out the window, although Fergus was pretty sure she wasn't actually looking at the neatly arranged garden and lawns outside. 'You're even more of an un-principled bastard than I thought you were.' She shook her head disbelievingly.

Fergus's mouth tightened at the deliberate insult. But what he had to remember was that it *was* deliberate; Chloe was hoping to anger him into refusing her father's dinner invitation.

'"Sticks and stones..."' he murmured tauntingly.

She turned back in turn. 'That's not all I would like to throw at you at the moment!'

He could see that; her hands were clenched into fists at her sides, her whole body tense with that frustrated fury.

And what Fergus most wanted to do at this moment was take her in his arms and kiss her!

But he didn't doubt, if he even attempted to do that, she really would hit him!

He gave her a casual smile. 'No doubt I can get the details for this evening from your father later—'

'Fergus, I really can't allow you to come out to dinner with my family,' she cut in determinedly. 'I shall have to tell my father—'

'Tell him what?' Fergus challenged. 'Exactly what do you intend telling your father about our friendship, Chloe? Are you going to tell him how you deliberately approached me two weeks ago?' he continued as she would have interrupted. 'That you spent that night at my home?' Fergus paused for a moment. 'Somehow I think not, Chloe,' he murmured as she visibly paled.

'I— You— I hate you!' Her eyes glittered with the emotion.

'I'm told there's a very thin line between hate and love,' he offered.

Although inwardly he wasn't quite so unshaken by the outburst. He didn't want Chloe to hate him. He wasn't sure what he wanted from her yet, but it certainly wasn't hate.

'I can assure you, that's a line I'll never cross!' She marched past him to the door, wrenching it open before turning to glare at him. 'You are, without doubt, the most despicable man I have ever met!'

God, she was so young. So tiny. So vulnerable. So much so that Fergus wanted to wrap her up in his arms and stop anything ever hurting her again.

What stopped him doing exactly that was that he might have a little trouble, when he went to see her father in a few minutes, explaining the obviously fresh scratch marks down his face!

'I'll see you this evening, Chloe,' he said instead.

Her mouth tightened. 'Perhaps I'll have a headache and not make the dinner tonight; I can definitely feel one coming on!'

Fergus raised mocking brows. 'Another one? I don't think you would do that to your sister and brother-in-law.'

Her shoulders slumped dejectedly. 'You're right, I wouldn't,' she conceded heavily, her eyes huge pools of pained disillusion as she looked up at him. 'One thing I do wish, Fergus McCloud—I wish that I had never met you,' she told him dully.

That barb definitely went home, and it took all Fergus's iron self-control not to go after her as she walked down the hallway, quietly letting herself out of the house before closing the door firmly behind her.

A nerve pulsed erratically in the hardness of Fergus's firmly set jaw as he watched her leave. He almost preferred her more dramatic departure of Tuesday lunchtime—at least then she hadn't actually told him she hated him!

But there was no doubting that her abrupt departure now left him in a bit of a predicament; he had absolutely no idea where Paul Hamilton's study was, and he certainly couldn't go wandering around the house looking for it, either!

'Can I help you? You're looking rather lost.'

Fergus had turned sharply at the sound of that husky female voice, feeling a jolt in his chest as he found himself looking at Chloe as she would be in thirty years or so. Tiny. Dark-haired. Delicately beautiful. Only fine lines beside the eyes and mouth to show for those extra thirty years of laughter and tears.

He knew who the woman was, of course. Diana, Chloe's mother.

'Mrs Hamilton,' he greeted politely. 'I'm supposed to be in your husband's study, and I'm afraid I got rather lost.' There was no point in explaining Chloe had just walked out and left him to fend for himself.

Diana laughed sympathetically. 'This house can be a bit confusing,' she allowed. 'Come with me,' she invited warmly, turning to lead the way down the carpeted hallway.

Fergus went—with the distinct feeling that not too many men would feel inclined to refuse such an invitation from this beautifully gracious woman!

He had seen photographs of her too, years ago in the newspapers, when her husband had been a big political figure, and more recently in his own research file, but none of those had prepared him for the open warmth and obvious beauty of the woman herself.

'Ah, Mr McCloud.' Paul Hamilton stood up at his entrance to his study, the smile he directed at his wife full of affection. 'Could you ask Mrs Harmon to send in some coffee for us, darling?' he requested.

'Of course,' Diana agreed smoothly. 'Nice to have met you, Mr McCloud.' She gave him a smile in parting, closing the door softly behind her.

'Please, do sit down.' Fergus's host indicated the chair opposite his at the huge mahogany desk. 'I didn't mention to Diana that she might see you again later this evening.' He smiled. 'Just in case you and Chloe didn't manage to sort things out to your mutual satisfaction.'

Fergus shrugged ruefully; he had sorted things out to his own satisfaction, even if it wasn't to Chloe's. 'I would love to join you all for dinner—as long as you're sure I'm not intruding?'

'Not at all,' Paul Hamilton assured him. 'Six is always a much rounder number than five.'

The fact that it had originally been five pleased Fergus immensely; at least it proved Chloe didn't already have anyone important enough in her life to have invited to this family celebration.

Although, having now met both Paul Hamilton and his wife, Diana, Fergus had to admit he felt the beginnings of unease in the pit of his stomach. Mainly, he could at least admit to himself, because he was starting to question whether or not Paul could possibly have ever been unfaithful to such a warmly beautiful woman as Diana undoubtedly was...

*   *   *

He dared, Chloe acknowledged disgustedly, glaring furiously across the room at Fergus as he was shown into the sitting-room later that evening, the family all gathered in there to have a glass of champagne prior to leaving for the restaurant.

She had no idea how Fergus's interview with her father had gone, had only seen her father for a few minutes on her return from shopping. But he hadn't seemed particularly disturbed.

Although Chloe couldn't say she'd felt the same way once he had told her that Fergus would be meeting them here at eight o'clock this evening!

'For goodness' sake, smile,' Fergus told her, having crossed to her side, a glass of champagne already in his hand, looking very handsome and distinguished in his black dinner suit. 'Your family will think you don't want me here,' he warned.

Chloe looked up at him with wary eyes, making no effort to hide her hostility. 'I don't,' she snapped.

Fergus laughed softly. 'Let's try not to spoil this evening for your sister and her husband,' he responded, before bending to kiss her lightly on the cheek. 'Window-dressing,' he explained before she could flinch away.

Her eyes sparkled angrily. 'Don't try and use me to get to my father or my family,' she grated.

His gaze hardened. 'I didn't mean that sort of window-dressing, Chloe,' he rasped, drawing a steadying breath before turning to look at the others gathered in the room. 'Don't you think you should introduce me to your sister and her husband?'

'No,' she answered flatly.

She didn't think he should be here at all. That was the whole problem. And if he couldn't see that—

'Chloe,' he began, slowly turning back to face her, 'if you recall I asked to have dinner with *you* this evening; your family's involvement is purely incidental.'

'Really?' she derided scornfully.

'Really,' he echoed hardly, his hand that wasn't holding the champagne glass reaching out to firmly grasp her forearm as he turned her to face him. 'I don't work that way, Chloe. And you can believe that or not, it's your choice.'

She was so angry with him at the moment that she couldn't even think straight, let alone make any choices!

He had no right to be here, socially mixing with her family as if he were a close friend of hers. That was what hurt the most; no matter what he might try to claim to the contrary, Fergus was merely using her.

'I choose not,' she told him coldly, bending to put down her empty champagne glass on the nearby coffee-table.

Fergus eyed the glass with raised brows. 'I thought you didn't drink...?'

Her mouth thinned humourlessly. 'For some strange reason, this evening I feel in need of it! In fact,' she bit out caustically, 'I think I'll have a refill!' She picked up her glass and crossed the room to where her father was just refilling Penny's glass.

Older than Chloe by ten years, Penny was more like their father, tall and elegant, her dark hair boyishly short, three pregnancies having done little to diminish the slenderness of her body.

'Twelve years, Pen,' Chloe teased, making a decided effort to shake off her anger towards Fergus; after all, this was Penny and David's evening. 'You'll be getting your long-service medal soon!'

Penny laughed, shooting an affectionate smile at her husband as he strolled over to chat to Fergus. 'And when can we expect to hear wedding bells from you...?' her sister prompted pointedly.

It took great effort to keep the smile on her own lips. Damn Fergus. Didn't he realise his presence here tonight would cause speculation amongst her family? Or did he just not care? That was probably closer to the truth!

'I'm not sure I'm the marrying kind,' Chloe replied with a noncommittal shrug.

'We all say that—usually just before we fall flat on our face in love!' her sister said knowingly.

'Not this girl,' Chloe assured with certainty, deciding it was high time—despite the fact that she had no real wish to spend time with Fergus herself!—that she interrupted his conversation with David. Or who knew what family confidences David might reveal without meaning to? 'If you'll excuse me...' she said before strolling over to join the two men.

David turned to give her a cheerful smile. 'I had no idea you knew such a famous writer,

Chloe,' he reproved lightly, the teasing lift of his brows seeming to ask if Fergus could possibly be the reason she had crept into the house last Saturday morning still wearing her evening dress from the night before.

Or was that just Chloe's imagination? Her own guilty conscience at work?

'A girl has to have some secrets from her family,' she countered brightly.

'But I'm not a secret any longer,' Fergus put in.

Chloe started visibly as she felt his arm drape lightly about her shoulders. Proprietorially. A pure act of possession.

Forget it, Fergus McCloud, Chloe fumed inwardly. One dinner, and then he was out of her life. For good!

'Isn't it time we were all moving on to the restaurant?' she suggested, using the act of putting her glass down on the table to escape that arm about her shoulders, easily meeting the challenge in his dark brown eyes as she looked up and found Fergus looking at her with amusement.

Challenge away, Fergus; her own gaze shot the message back at him. His time for calling the shots came to an end the moment this evening did!

'I think it's been decided that the two of us will travel in my car, and the others will go in your father's car,' Fergus told her with obvious satisfaction.

Decided by whom? She didn't remember being party to such a conversation. She—

'Is that okay with you, Chloe?' David was the one to ask her politely, seeming to have picked up a little on her mood.

'Absolutely fine,' she assured him airily—it would give her a chance to tell Fergus exactly what she would and wouldn't accept about his presence here this evening. Having him lay claim to her in such an obvious way was definitely unacceptable.

She was totally unprepared, once they all got outside, for the fact that Fergus's car was a dark-grey-coloured replica of her own!

'Odd, isn't it?' Fergus observed as he pressed the button to unlock the doors.

Chloe instantly damped down her surprise, shrugging dismissively as she got into the passenger seat. 'Not particularly,' she said as he got in beside her. 'It just proves that on certain subjects you have good judgement!'

Fergus chuckled softly. 'But only on certain subjects, hmm,' he acknowledged wryly.

Chloe didn't even qualify the statement with an answer, sitting silently at his side as he manoeuvred the car to follow behind her father's to the restaurant.

But that wasn't to say she wasn't completely aware of Fergus. Much more so than she wanted to be. And more so than she wanted to admit!

Why him? The very last man she should find herself attracted to!

Because she *was* attracted to him. Half the anger she had directed at him already tonight had been because the moment he'd walked into the sitting-room she had been aware of him. It had been as if all her nerve endings had suddenly come tinglingly alive, each and every one of them finely attuned to Fergus McCloud.

'What are you thinking about?' Fergus suddenly asked.

Chloe instantly tensed, wondering if her expression could possibly have given away any of her disturbed thoughts. She certainly hoped not!

'I was wondering what poison would be the least detectable when given in food,' she answered with saccharine sweetness.

Fergus chuckled. 'I don't think I've told you yet how beautiful you look tonight,' he said admiringly.

'In this particular case, Fergus, flattery will get you nowhere!' she told him tautly.

But she couldn't help feeling pleased that her effort to look good this evening had obviously paid off. Her figure-hugging, knee-length silk dress was the colour of pale milky coffee, perfectly complementing the tan she had acquired earlier in the summer, her long hair looking almost black against the light-coloured material, her make-up kept to a glowing minimum, peach-coloured gloss enhancing her lips

'I'm not trying to ''get'' anywhere, Chloe,' Fergus told her wearily. 'Could we not just agree to drop hostilities for this evening—all coming from your side, I might add!—and enjoy a nice dinner with your family?'

No, they could not! She daredn't let down her guard when around Fergus McCloud. And not just because of what he was trying to do to her father...

She was very much afraid she had fallen in love with the enemy!

CHAPTER NINE

'I'M NOT the enemy, Chloe,' Fergus told her grimly, very aware that she certainly regarded him as such. 'In fact,' he continued carefully, 'I would like to talk to you later. Alone. I have a proposal to put to you.'

She gave him a startled look. 'A what?'

Fergus smiled humourlessly at her obvious shock. 'Not that sort of proposal, Chloe,' he corrected. 'A suggestion. An idea I have that might help both of us,' he enlarged.

Chloe looked scathing now. 'Why do I have the feeling I'm not going to like this idea?'

'Probably because at the moment you don't particularly like anything about me?'

'I wouldn't have clarified that remark with at the moment,' she told him flatly, turning to uncooperatively look out of the side window.

Fergus couldn't help but smile at her candidness. Although…come to think of it, what she had said wasn't that funny, he realised. Did she really not like him at all? In the circumstances, he couldn't exactly say he blamed her, but that didn't make the fact any more palatable.

'Your father doesn't share your dislike of me,' he pointed out.

'No,' Chloe acknowledged guardedly. 'Why is that?'

'Probably because when I told him I was researching a political thriller, I omitted to mention the subject of Susan Stirling,' Fergus admitted grimly.

Chloe turned to him searchingly, looking totally nonplussed by his statement. 'I don't understand,' she finally responded.

Neither did he. Not completely. Oh, he had been shaken slightly earlier in the week by Chloe's complete belief in her father's innocence, but he had also known that, in the circumstances, her loyalty was understandable.

But meeting Paul Hamilton today, listening for over an hour to what he was sure was the man's complete candidness in answer to his questions, Fergus hadn't felt able to broach the subject of the scandal that had brought the other man's political career to a halt eight years ago. Especially when Paul was so obviously thrilled with his decision to re-enter the political arena.

Fergus knew that his wife, Diana's, likeness to Chloe could also have had something to do with his reluctance to alienate the other man...

'I'm reserving judgement, okay,' he rejoined impatiently.

But he could feel Chloe's gaze was still on him, as if she might read something else from his expression. She wouldn't. Before concentrating full time on writing, he had been a practising lawyer for over five years, had learnt only too well how to mask his inner emotions.

Besides, he wasn't a hundred-per-cent certain what his emotions were at the moment. On one level he was angry with himself for chickening out during his meeting with Paul Hamilton this morning. But, on another level, he knew that if he hadn't made that last-minute decision, he certainly wouldn't be here with Chloe now.

Finally she drew in a long breath. 'How big of you,' she said contemptuously, obviously not impressed.

He couldn't help that; at the moment it was as far as he was willing to go on that particular subject. 'I thought so,' he acknowledged dryly. 'The important thing is, are you willing to do the same?' He quirked dark brows as he kept his gaze on the road ahead.

'Concerning what?' she returned guardedly.

'Concerning dinner, of course. As far as your family are aware, I'm only here this evening as your partner. Can we leave it at that for the moment?'

'That really depends on you—doesn't it?' she countered.

He sighed deeply. 'I'm hardly likely to ask any embarrassing questions in front of your mother!' There was no way he could deliberately hurt the graciously lovely Diana!

'I suppose that's something to be grateful for!' Chloe exclaimed disgustedly.

Fergus gave up trying to reason with her, concentrating on following Paul Hamilton's car to the restaurant. He was satisfied that, for the moment, Chloe wasn't going to give away his ulterior motive for seeing her father this morning; if she had been going to do that, then she already would have done it!

It didn't need too much time spent in their company to see the Hamiltons were a close family, Fergus realised once he was seated with them at the table and they had ordered their meal. There was a playful warmth

amongst them all that spoke of affectionate fa-
miliarity.

Fergus had shared a happy camaraderie with
his two cousins as he'd grown up in Scotland
after his parents' divorce, and his grandfather
had shown them all a taciturn affection. But
there had never been any of the teasing and
laughter over their meals that the Hamiltons
obviously enjoyed together.

If this evening was doing nothing else, it
was showing him exactly why Chloe had tried
to intercede with him on her father's behalf.
Even if her method had been more than a little
lacking in judgement!

'My husband tells me you're in the middle
of writing a political thriller, Mr McCloud?'
Mrs Hamilton prompted interestedly.

He didn't even need to glance Chloe's way
to know of her tension as she obviously overheard the question. Damn it, didn't she believe
him when he told her he was here for no other
reason than to have dinner with her?
Obviously not, he accepted irritably, after the
briefest of glimpses at her rigidly set expression.

He turned to smile at Diana. 'Please call me
Fergus,' he invited smoothly. 'And in the mid-

dle of writing is a slight exaggeration; I'm still heavily into the research,' he admitted.

'Do you have to do much of that?' Diana asked interestedly.

Fergus found himself relaxing totally as he talked to Chloe's mother. There was no doubting that Diana made a good politician's wife; she had a way of putting one at one's ease, while at the same time showing genuine interest in what was being said.

'For goodness' sake,' Chloe hissed at him ten minutes later, having exhausted, for the moment, her own conversation with David Lantham, who sat on her other side. 'My mother was only being polite,' she snapped once she had Fergus's full attention. 'You didn't have to give her a step-by-step account of your research process!' Her eyes flashed deeply blue.

Fergus looked at her searchingly for several long seconds, head tilted on one side, unrelenting in that reproachful gaze until he saw the uncomfortable colour that entered her cheeks.

'That's better,' he murmured with satisfaction. 'What would you rather I talked to your mother about?' he taunted, aware that the others seated at the table were deep in a political conversation.

Chloe glared at him now. 'I would rather you didn't talk to her at all!'

'Not very practical, in the circumstances,' he drawled. 'Besides, I like your mother, and there's no way I could be rude to her.'

'I— You— Oh, eat your prawns!' Chloe muttered with obvious frustration, putting down her fork as she gave up any attempt to eat any more of the whitebait she had ordered as her own starter.

Fergus reached out and lightly covered one of her hands with his own. 'Just relax, Chloe,' he advised gently. 'I'm not here tonight as Fergus McCloud, writer.'

'Then what are you here as?' she scorned.

'Fergus McCloud, lover?' He raised mocking dark brows.

The colour deepened in her cheeks even as she drew in an angry breath. 'I've already told you that we didn't—'

'Wishful thinking on my part?' he cut in. 'For the future,' he added huskily.

That had the power of totally silencing her, Fergus noted with satisfaction, her mouth opening and shutting like a goldfish's in a bowl. Although it also had the effect of Chloe snatching her hand from beneath his, and hiding both hands under the table. Which didn't please him at all...

He chuckled. 'You really are incredibly sweet, Chloe,' he told her warmly.

'You make me sound as if I'm ten years old!' she came back disgruntledly.

Fergus smiled. 'Sometimes you behave as if you were. But not too often,' he amended as she would have retorted again. 'I think the next few weeks could be rather fun...' he said enigmatically.

Whatever did he mean by that remark...?

And that other one—wishful thinking for the future...!

If he thought she was going to go on seeing him, while at the same time he made every effort to gather information that was going to disgrace her father, then he was in for a nasty surprise!

Surely Fergus couldn't be that insensitive?

He was obviously slightly bemused by the teasing and cajoling that went on amongst her family, and she believed him when he said he liked her mother. But none of that changed the fact that he intended writing a book that would throw the Hamiltons into turmoil all over again.

Perhaps he was *that* insensitive, after all...

She was also slightly bemused herself by that proposal he had mentioned in the car on the way here. If it had anything to do with the two of them continuing to see each other, then he could just forget it. There was absolutely no way she could agree to do that.

Although it wouldn't necessarily be because she didn't want to...

That alive feeling she had experienced earlier this evening when he'd arrived had continued to stay with her, so much so that she was aware of every movement he made, every word that he said. Her hand still tingled from where he had touched it minutes ago!

In truth, her chagrin at his lengthy conversation with her mother wasn't completely because she thought he was being duplicitous; she had jealously resented every smile, every word, he had directed at Diana.

Was this what being in love with someone was like? Feeling jealous of your own mother because the man you loved could talk more easily with her than he could with you? Or was it just that she knew Fergus didn't return that love…?

What good would it do her, would it do either of them, if he did fall in love with her? Nothing could change the fact that he had the power to destroy her family. Something she could never, ever forgive him for.

'You're looking very serious all of a sudden.' Fergus looked at her searchingly now. 'What are you thinking about?'

The same thing she had thought about constantly for the last two weeks—him!

Chloe gave him a scathing glance. 'My thoughts—thank goodness!—have always been completely my own!'

He nodded consideringly. 'I've never really thought about it before, but it can't have been easy growing up in your father's political spotlight.'

She stiffened resentfully. 'I thought you weren't going to discuss that this evening,' she reminded him.

'I never said I wouldn't talk about you.' He sighed impatiently.

Chloe smiled humourlessly. 'I'm my father's daughter.'

Fergus gave a sardonic smile back. 'You're a damn sight more than that!'

She quirked dark brows. 'Am I?' she prompted. Not sure that she was. To him, at least.

His eyes narrowed. 'Do you know what I really want to do at this moment...?'

Chloe eyed him warily, not sure she wanted to know the answer to that. 'Smack my backside,' she guessed slowly.

'I've thought about it,' he admitted with a grin. 'But my grandfather brought us all up, Logan, Brice, and myself, to treat women with a certain respect,' he explained. 'I think that rules out smacking their bottoms!'

She grinned. 'Your grandfather sounds like a very sensible man to me.'

Fergus returned her grin. 'Actually, he's an old devil. But I don't doubt that he would like you. No, Chloe, what I really want to do right now is kiss you,' he continued conversationally. 'Preferably until you're senseless. Or, at least, silent!' he added ruefully.

'It's sometimes the only way where women are concerned!' her father was the one to answer Fergus laughingly.

Chloe turned self-consciously to find that all her family were looking at them, her cheeks blushing bright red as she wondered exactly how long they had been listening to the barbed conversation between Fergus and herself. Obviously not long enough for them to have heard her earlier accusations, or they wouldn't all be smiling so indulgently!

'Please, Daddy, Fergus needs no encouragement in being outrageous!' she reproved lightly, doing her best to minimalise the importance of Fergus claiming he wanted to kiss her until she was senseless—or silent. Even if just the thought of it made her tremble with longing!

'Obviously not,' her father responded approvingly.

That approval of Fergus, by all her family, became even more apparent as the evening progressed.

Not that Chloe could exactly blame them. Fergus had an array of amusing stories to entertain them all with, was very charming and attentive to all the Hamilton women—something else his grandfather had no doubt instilled in him. In fact, Fergus was the ideal dinner guest!

'What's wrong now?' Fergus asked wearily as he drove the two of them back to her home at the end of the evening.

Chloe snapped out of the reverie she had fallen into the last few minutes, turning to look at him as she realised she must have been frowning. 'Truthfully?' she returned dully.

'It's always preferable to a lie—no matter how politely it's given,' he confirmed wryly.

She sighed. 'I was wishing you were anyone else but who you really are,' she admitted candidly.

It was Fergus's turn to look serious. 'Explain, please,' he bit out.

She wasn't sure that she could. Not without revealing exactly how emotionally involved she had become with him without really meaning to.

'I actually quite like you, Fergus,' she began cautiously.

'Careful, Chloe,' he taunted. 'Let's not get too effusive!'

She gave him an impatient glance. 'Don't worry—I don't intend to,' she assured him. 'I like you, and under any other circumstances, I might even enjoy your company,' she told him grudgingly. 'But as it is...'

'As I told you earlier, Chloe, I am not the enemy,' he cut in tersely.

'Can't you see that to me that's exactly what you are?' she came back fiercely, her hands tightly clenched.

'I also mentioned earlier that I want to talk to you,' he ground out, his hands gripping the steering wheel. 'Is there anywhere we can go so we can talk privately?'

Chloe thought for a minute. No doubt Penny and David would stay and have a nightcap once they reached her parents' home, which ruled that out. And, as she shared that home with her parents... But going to Fergus's home was just as unacceptable; she would then be totally reliant on Fergus to drive her home after they had talked.

'Drop me off at home so that I can drive over to your house,' she said flatly. 'I presume we can talk privately there?'

'We can...yes,' he replied slowly. 'I only said I would like to kiss you until you're senseless, Chloe; that doesn't mean I'm going to!'

'You won't be given the chance to,' she assured him with certainty.

Fergus shot her a narrow-eyed glance before turning his attention back to the road.

But his anger was a tangible thing, the relaxed atmosphere that had developed over their meal completely dissipated.

However, Chloe couldn't help that. She had to keep this man at arm's length; she had no choice. No matter how much she might wish it were otherwise!

It took her only a couple of minutes, once she reached the house, to say goodnight to her parents, Penny and David, collect her car keys, and set off to join Fergus at his home. Having already said goodnight to her family at the restaurant, Fergus had driven off as soon as Chloe had got out of his car, the angry set to his features telling her he'd still been far from happy about the arrangement.

Tough. This suited her much better, and, where Fergus was concerned, she knew she had to maintain her independence.

The lights were on in the house when she pulled her car up onto the driveway, Fergus answering the door after her first ring, offering no greeting, looking completely unapproachable as he led the way through to the sitting-room.

'Brandy?' he offered tersely, having already poured one for himself before she arrived.

'Not when I'm driving, thank you,' she refused as she steadily met his gaze across the room and sat down in one of the armchairs.

Fergus took a sip of his own brandy, grimacing slightly as the alcohol hit the back of his throat. 'Hear me out first, hmm?' he finally said. 'And don't get defensive at my first comment.'

She raised dark brows. 'Surely that depends on what you have to say?'

He began to pace the room, his height and presence totally dominating.

But Chloe refused to feel intimidated, sensing Fergus's own uncertainty with what he was about to say.

Finally he came to an abrupt halt, turning to face her, his expression grim. 'I know who told you about my book, Chloe.'

Her gaze didn't waver, but she could feel the colour receding from her cheeks. 'How?' she croaked.

His mouth thinned humourlessly. 'Process of elimination,' he explained. 'My agent's talks with the publisher were only verbal, and only with my editor, so that was pretty much a dead end. Which brought me back to the agent himself. Bernie is many things,' he acknowledged dryly, 'but indiscreet is not one of them. He has an assistant and a secretary, the former being female, and as ambitious as Bernie himself. Besides, Stella Whitney does not strike me as a woman who indulges in girlish confidences! Which only left the secretary,' he concluded.

Chloe was barely breathing—how could she, when her heart was in her mouth?

Fergus looked grim. 'I didn't have to dig too deeply to discover that Victoria Pelman, coincidentally, is your cousin. The daughter of your mother's sister.' He looked at Chloe with raised brows.

She swallowed hard, moistening suddenly dry lips. Victoria had been in a terrible state when Chloe had met her for lunch five weeks ago, obviously having needed to tell Chloe something, but at the same time having been aware that it had been a professional confidence she shouldn't have shared. With anyone. Family loyalty had—fortunately for Chloe!—won out.

'What do you mean to do with that information?' she prompted Fergus hollowly.

'What do you think I should do with it?'

Chloe grimaced. What she would really like was for him to just forget he had ever found out about it. But she doubted that was about to happen.

'Victoria acted in good faith,' she defended.

'It isn't her motivation that's in question,' Fergus rasped.

Chloe stood up, now feeling at too much of a disadvantage as she sat in the armchair. 'If it had been you, or one of your cousins, who had discovered something that could hurt someone in your family, what would you have expected them to do about it?' she challenged.

'Exactly the same as Victoria did,' he acknowledged heavily. 'But, unfortunately, that doesn't really solve this present dilemma for me—does it?'

No, she could see that, Chloe accepted. But she and Victoria were the same age, had grown up together. During their childhood years the two girls had spent almost as much time in each other's homes as they had their own.

Of course, their lives had taken separate paths as they'd reached adulthood, but the two women were no less close because of that. Victoria might love her job as secretary to

Bernard Crosby. It was just that she loved her family more.

Chloe drew in a shaky breath. 'I ask you again, what do you mean to do with that information?'

She had tried so hard to keep Victoria's involvement out of this situation, had hoped—futilely!—that Fergus would be so caught up in the fact that Chloe knew so much about him and his proposed book that he wouldn't actually question how she knew.

Fergus's gaze was narrowed on the paleness of her face, his mouth twisting hardly as he seemed to guess at least some of her thoughts. 'I'm sure you and your cousin have had a great time discussing my private life—'

'We didn't—well...not in the way you're implying,' Chloe amended awkwardly.

'I think knowing a detail like how I take my coffee comes under the heading of my private life,' he drawled. 'Don't you?'

'Don't be ridiculous,' Chloe snapped to cover her own discomfort. 'Apparently Victoria has made you coffee at least a dozen times during your appointments with your agent.'

'Probably,' Fergus conceded. 'But my address and telephone number definitely come under the heading of privileged information!'

Chloe winced at the justified attack. 'I didn't use either of them; until after I had actually met you at the nightclub,' she replied.

'To your credit, no, you didn't,' he agreed wearily.

Nevertheless, Chloe didn't take any comfort from the admission, sensing Fergus was far from finished. 'How long have you known?'

'A couple of days.'

But he had waited until now to confront her with it. There was also the fact that he had arrived for his appointment with her father this morning with the intention of inviting her out to lunch with him today...

'What do you want, Fergus?' she asked tonelessly.

His head went back. 'What makes you think I want anything?'

She smiled without humour. 'The fact that I stopped believing in Father Christmas and the Tooth Fairy years ago!'

The last thing she wanted to do was endanger Victoria's job with Bernard Crosby. And if Fergus's own family loyalty was anything like her own, and she thought it probably was, then he was going to know that about her too.

'Your idea, Fergus?' she prompted hardly, referring to his remark at the beginning of the evening, even more sure now that she wasn't going to like this idea.

'I want you to help me with the research for my book,' he stated evenly.

Chloe stared at him. He couldn't be serious!

But she could see by his unwavering gaze, his unsmiling mouth, the inflexibility of his jaw, that he was. Deadly serious!

CHAPTER TEN

CHLOE, Fergus realised in the split second before her hand slowly began to rise from her side, was going to hit him!

He reached out and easily grasped the wrist of that threatening hand. 'I don't think so, Chloe,' he warned.

She struggled in that grasp, her face suffused with angry colour. 'You bastard!' she gasped. 'You scheming—'

'*I'm* scheming?' he echoed incredulously.

'—blackmailing—'

'Stop right there, Chloe,' he bit out harshly, his hand tightening on her wrist. 'Before you say something we're both going to regret!'

She glared up at him, breathing hard. '*I* won't regret it!'

'I don't know what context you've put on my idea—although, from your reaction, I can guess!' he rasped disgustedly. 'But I am most definitely not suggesting an exchange, my silence about Victoria's involvement for information on your father and Susan Stirling.' He was angry himself now. Furiously so. 'If I were the type of man to want something in exchange for my silence, you can be assured I would be likely to ask something from you of a much more intimate nature than that!'

Chloe became suddenly still, her only movement now the quick rise and fall of her breasts as she breathed deeply in her agitation, the colour slowly draining from her cheeks. She looked, Fergus acknowledged achingly, absolutely beautiful!

She swallowed hard. 'I think asking me to betray my own father is quite intimate enough!' she exclaimed distastefully.

'I don't want you to betray your father, damn it,' Fergus snapped impatiently. 'Hell, Chloe, you certainly aren't making this easy for me.' He shook his head frustratedly.

She glared up at him, her face only inches away from his own. 'And I never will,' she assured him determinedly.

This wasn't the time. Fergus knew it wasn't. It could only make the situation between them worse than it already was. But for the moment, her perfume invading his senses, her warm closeness totally arousing, he just couldn't stop himself. He bent his head and kissed her.

For stunned seconds she stood completely still, but as he released her wrist, his arms moving about the slenderness of her waist, she was galvanised into action.

But as she tried to wrench her mouth from his Fergus moved one of his hands behind her head, resisting the movement, the struggles of her body against his, as he moulded her against him, doing nothing to lessen his sudden desire for her.

She tasted so good as he sipped and tasted her mouth, felt so right in his arms, his own body alive with wanting her.

All evening he had sat and watched her as she'd talked and laughed with her family, wishing she could be that relaxed and happy with him, but inwardly knowing that all he could have was this. Chloe might try to deny that she responded to him, but he knew differently; on this level the two of them were in complete accord.

And, for this moment, this was all there was...

Chloe was no longer fighting him, her mouth moving hungrily against his, her fingers threaded in the dark thickness of his hair, the softness of her breasts pressing against the hardness of his chest.

Fergus knew that he wanted her. Wanted desperately to make love to her. To lay her down on the carpeted floor and lose himself completely in the scented softness of her body.

But if he did that now he knew he would be no better than she had accused him of being. Worse, that he would lose her for ever.

It wasn't easy dragging his mouth from hers, in fact it was probably the hardest thing he had ever had to do in his life. But he did it none-theless, his hands moving so that he now cra-dled her heated cheeks. If they didn't, he might have allowed himself to touch the softness of her breasts—and then he wouldn't have been *able* to stop!

'I want you to work with me, Chloe,' he told her gruffly. 'Not against your father, but *for* him,' he continued firmly as she would have spoken.

Her gaze was slightly unfocused as she blinked up at him. 'I don't understand,' she murmured huskily.

Fergus drew in a sharp breath. 'I told you, I'm reserving judgement,' he reminded softly.

'You maintain your father wasn't involved with Susan Stirling—'

'He wasn't,' she cut in.

'Or the father of her child,' Fergus continued determinedly. 'But someone was. Obviously,' he added dryly. 'If we can find out who that someone was—'

'We?' Chloe echoed scathingly.

Fergus's hands dropped from her face as he moved abruptly away from her; he couldn't think straight when he was that close to Chloe. 'I'm willing to make a deal with you, Chloe,' he said sharply. 'If, in the course of our research, we discover that there was another man, then I'll hold up my hands and admit I was wrong, okay?'

She stared at him with hard blue eyes. 'And if we don't discover ''another man''?' she prompted scornfully. 'After all, why should we? The police did their own investigation after Susan's death, and they couldn't find any involvement at all. Which fuelled the rumours even more,' she added bitterly.

Fergus was well aware of that. But, hard as he had tried, he couldn't think of any other way round this problem. If they could find this other man, maybe Chloe would stop hating him...

His eyes narrowed. 'You called her Susan... Did you know her?'

Chloe turned away. 'Of course I knew her. She worked for my father. Eight years ago she was at the house practically all the time.'

Somehow that fact had never occurred to Fergus. There were a lot of things about this situation that had never occurred to him! In fact, he was beginning to wish he had never involved himself with that scandal eight years ago.

Although, if he hadn't, he would probably never have met Chloe at all...

He gave Chloe a considering look. 'What did you think of her?'

Chloe turned back angrily. 'I was fifteen years old; what do you think I thought of her?'

'Most fifteen-year-old girls nowadays seem very—um—probably ''worldly'' is the best word to use,' he grimaced thoughtfully.

'Well, I wasn't,' Chloe snapped. 'I was away at boarding-school most of the time, anyway. Susan just seemed—she was over thirty—she just seemed old to me!'

Fergus smiled grimly. Probably in the same way he, at thirty-five, now seemed old to her! 'But you must have formed some impression of her, surely?' he persisted doggedly.

'Okay,' she sighed her impatience. 'Susan was beautiful. Very beautiful, in fact. Is that what you wanted to hear?' Her eyes sparkled deeply blue.

Not particularly. As with Chloe's parents, he also already knew what Susan Stirling looked like. He was more interested in what sort of person she had been.

'You didn't answer my question, Fergus,' Chloe bit out tautly. 'What happens if you can't find another man for Susan to have been involved with?'

That was something he hoped wouldn't happen! It would totally ruin his storyline if they did find another man, but Fergus knew that would now be preferable to him to having Chloe learn that she had been wrong about her father all along...!

'We would be working on the basis that there is another man.'

Chloe shook her head. 'There is no we, Fergus,' she said hardly. 'I don't intend helping you to hammer any more nails in my father's political coffin.'

'I'm not trying to do that,' he came back frustratedly. 'Damn it, I'm trying to help your father, not harm him!' And, at the same time, he hoped to spend some time with Chloe, help her to see that he really wasn't the bad guy.

'I can't help you, Fergus,' she told him flatly.

She really was the most stubborn—! 'What about Victoria? Your cousin,' he reminded her.

Her mouth turned down humourlessly. 'I know who she is, Fergus.' She sighed again heavily. 'I don't know. All I do know is that I can't help you.'

'Won't, Chloe,' Fergus responded tautly. 'In this case, there's a vast difference between can't and won't. The truth of the matter is, you don't trust me, do you, Chloe?' His gaze was concentrated on the paleness of her face.

She returned that gaze for several long seconds, finally looking away. 'I have very little reason to trust you—'

'You've given me even less reason to trust *you*,' he cut in. 'But doesn't the fact that I'm offering to work alongside you in this show that I'm willing to do just that?'

'It shows you're willing to let me help you to continue to deceive my family into trusting you—'

'Damn it, I don't remember even mentioning your family!' His eyes blazed furiously.

'You don't need to; how else do you intend finding out the truth? No, Fergus, if I were interested in having anyone as Dr Watson to my Sherlock Holmes, you can be assured you would not be in the running!'

'Wrong billing there, Chloe; *I* would be Sherlock Holmes,' he contradicted with hard derision.

She smiled sadly. 'You see, we wouldn't even be able to agree on that—'

'We don't *have* to agree to discover the truth!' Fergus pushed determinedly. '"The truth shall make you free",' he quoted.

Chloe's smile was tremulous now. 'And some truth has to be taken on blind faith. The sort of faith I have in my father,' she added huskily.

Fergus couldn't argue with that. In fact, it was that faith, as well as the meeting with Paul Hamilton himself, that made him question his own earlier conviction that this had just been another case of a politician arrogantly breaking the unwritten rules of moral decency that his job as a public administrator insisted upon.

'Wouldn't it be better, for your father's re-entry into politics, if the whole situation had been cleared up, put away, and forgotten?' Fergus tried another approach.

'It would be better if the situation were left where it's been the last eight years—put away,' Chloe told him fiercely.

'But not forgotten,' Fergus pointed out softly.

'My answer is still no, Fergus,' she said firmly. 'I'm sorry, but that's the way it has to be.'

'It isn't the way it has to be. It's the way you've decided it should be.' He paused momentarily. 'Look, Chloe, I can either do this with you or without you. I would have preferred to do it with you.'

Her eyes widened. 'You're going to continue with your research, regardless?'

Fergus didn't particularly care for the distaste he could easily read in her expression. But he knew they had come too far along this route for him to be able to stop now.

He could agree right now not to write the book, but at the same time he knew, if he

wanted to continue to see Chloe, that, unre-
solved, it would always be between them. An
unmentioned shadow. And, above all else, no
matter how she might try to fight it, he knew
that he intended to continue seeing Chloe!

'I have no choice, Chloe,' he told her gently.

Her expression conveyed her disgust. 'You
have a choice, Fergus—you're just not taking
it! I should have known what sort of man you
were that first night I met you!' Her eyes were
glacially blue as they raked over him scornfully.

His hands clenched at his sides at her deliberately insulting tone, forcing himself to remember that was exactly what it was—deliberate. Chloe was determined to totally alienate
him. But, perversely, that very determination
gave him some sort of hope for the future. A
future that might include Chloe...

'Oh, but you did know what sort of man I
am, Chloe,' he murmured. 'Victoria told
you—remember?'

Colour heightened her cheeks. 'I think I had
better leave, Fergus,' she said stiffly. 'I don't
think we have anything further to say to each
other.'

He was silent, knowing that wasn't the case where he was concerned. But Chloe was probably right for the moment; she was too angry and upset right now to really listen to what he had to say.

'I'll walk you to the door,' he offered politely.

'Making sure I leave this time?' she taunted as she preceded him out of the room.

He didn't need any reminder of the night she had spent here without his knowledge—he had been kicking himself over it for the last two weeks!

'I would rather that you weren't leaving at all,' he assured her gruffly. 'But I accept that isn't even a possibility.' He smiled ruefully as she gave him a mocking glance.

'Goodbye, Fergus,' Chloe returned a bittersweet smile before getting into her car.

He felt his heart sink at the finality of her words. 'Good*night*, Chloe,' he said with emphasis. 'I'm sure I'll be seeing you again very soon.'

She didn't exactly look thrilled at the prospect, Fergus acknowledged as she drove away. But, hopefully, the next time he saw her, he would have better news to give her...

*   *   *

'How long have you known Fergus McCloud?'

Chloe frowned at David as she looked up from the design she had been working on for the last hour. 'Sorry?' She delayed answering him, instantly on the defensive at the mention of Fergus's name.

She had lived in dread the last three days, since dinner on Friday night, of one of her family questioning her about her supposed friendship with Fergus. Her parents had been understandingly quiet on the subject, perhaps suspecting a serious romance, and not wanting to pry until she was ready to talk about it herself. She hadn't seen or spoken to Penny since Friday—but, from David's interest now, her sister and her husband had obviously discussed the subject of herself and Fergus!

'I asked how long have you known Fergus McCloud?' David repeated.

She put down her pencil, smiling at her brother-in-law as he came fully into the room at the top of the house that had been converted into a studio for her, several overhead windows installed to give her better light to work in. 'A few weeks,' she replied casually. 'So you can tell Penny not to shop for a wedding outfit just yet!' she added with a lightness she was far from feeling.

The last three days had not been easy ones, part of her dreading any mention of Fergus by her family, the other half of her wondering what Fergus was doing, how much deeper he had gone with his research. And wondering if she should have been quite so vehement in her refusal to help him. Perhaps it would have been better to know what Fergus was doing rather than sit here in absolute darkness waiting for the axe to fall!

David didn't return her smile. 'In your father's absence, I've just taken a telephone call from the advisor to the Leader of the Opposition,' he said, concern in his tone. 'He had something of a personal nature that he thought your father should know about. Something Peter Ambrose felt your father should be made aware of without going through any official channels.'

Chloe felt a tight knot in her chest. 'Yes...?' she prompted, really only to give herself time to think.

Any mention of her father, Fergus McCloud, and Peter Ambrose in the same conversation could only mean one thing!

David looked grave. 'I don't want to hurt you, Chloe, but— Fergus McCloud wasn't exactly truthful when he came to see your father here last week. He forgot to mention that the political thriller he's thinking of writing is loosely based on the Susan Stirling scandal!' he revealed.

Chloe drew in a sharp breath; David certainly wasn't pulling any punches on this one! 'On what he believes to be the Susan Stirling scandal,' she corrected firmly. 'We all know that isn't what really happened.'

'Do we?' David retorted. 'Hell, Chloe— why on earth didn't you tell any of us what he was up to?' he groaned exasperatedly. 'Why did you let me find out from another source like this? More to the point, don't you realise that Fergus McCloud has been using you to get to your father?'

That wasn't strictly true; she doubted Fergus would have bothered getting to know her at all if she hadn't forced her company on him. But she wasn't about to tell David that; he was clearly annoyed with her enough already.

She stood up impatiently, feeling like a little girl being chastised by the headmaster. 'Of course I realise that,' she snapped back angrily.

'Why do you imagine I'm no longer seeing him?' Her eyes blazed across at him.

David rubbed a hand across his furrowed brow. 'How long have you known what he's up to? Apparently Peter saw you out to dinner with him some time ago.'

'Just over a week ago, actually,' she amended with irritation. 'And it's irrelevant how long I've known about the book.' She didn't intend bringing Victoria into this any more than she had to; it was bad enough that Fergus knew of her involvement! 'Fergus intends writing it.'

'There must be legal moves we can—'

'Fergus is a lawyer, David,' she told him solemnly. 'He knows exactly how far he can go on that narrow line between fact and fiction without ending up in court defending a libel suit.' As he had already assured her! 'The real problem, as I see it, is which one of us is going to break the news to my father?'

It was something she had been putting off doing herself, loath to burst her father's bubble of happiness at the thought of re-entering politics. Oh, he had continued to be successful at business the last eight years, but politics was what he was really good at. But now that Peter

Ambrose had unofficially issued a warning to her father, all idea of resurrecting her father's political career might have to be forgotten...

Damn Fergus McCloud, she thought, and not for the first time.

'I'll tell him,' David said grimly. 'Although he will probably want to talk to you afterwards,' he warned.

She expected that. Although she still had no idea what she was going to say...

'You say you've stopped seeing Fergus?' David said slowly.

'Most definitely,' she assured him.

'Are you sure that's a good idea...?' her brother-in-law commented thoughtfully.

Chloe shook her head impatiently. 'Make your mind up, David! In one breath you're berating me for having anything to do with the man, and in the next you're suggesting— Exactly what are you suggesting, David?' she asked warily.

'I don't know!' He ran an agitated hand through his thinning hair. 'I've been totally thrown by all of this. I can't think straight. I thought it was all over, that the past was dead and buried—'

'Along with Susan Stirling?' Chloe put in huskily.

David gave her a stunned look. 'That's a hell of a thing to say...'

She shrugged apologetically. 'You seemed to express some doubt earlier about my father's personal involvement with Susan.' She hadn't missed that earlier question mark when she'd asserted that they all knew the truth. 'Do you know something we don't?'

David gave her a sharp look. 'What do you mean?'

'Exactly what I said.' Chloe sighed, a sick feeling seeming to have settled in the pit of her stomach. 'You and Daddy have always been close, perhaps he confided in you when he couldn't confide in anyone else in the family—'

'Chloe, your father was not—absolutely not—involved with Susan Stirling,' David told her.

She heaved a sigh of relief. 'Nevertheless, he will have to be told about Fergus's book.'

'But maybe not yet,' David said. 'I would like to talk to Fergus myself before either of us say anything to your father.'

'He won't listen to you any more than he would listen to me,' she warned.

'Maybe not,' David accepted ruefully. 'But I still feel I have to try. Your father is a damned good politician, and he's already sacrificed enough to this mess.'

She was well aware of that, the whole family were. And she admired David for at least wanting to plead her father's case. She just knew he was wasting his time.

But Fergus had offered them one way out... At least, he had offered it to her...

'Could you just leave it for a few days, David?' she said at last. 'I would like to have one last try at reasoning with Fergus myself before anyone else gets involved,' she explained at David's frowning look.

'And what do I tell Peter Ambrose in the meantime?' David demanded.

'That the situation is under control?' she suggested, hoping that might be the case once she had pleaded her father's case just once more with Fergus.

But very much afraid that it wouldn't be...

CHAPTER ELEVEN

THE ringing doorbell was not a welcome interruption to Fergus's solitary dinner. Not that he was particularly enjoying the wonderful steak and kidney pudding Maud had prepared for him; he hadn't tasted a single mouthful he had eaten so far. He simply wasn't in the mood for company.

It had not been a good weekend after his unsatisfactory parting from Chloe on Friday evening, and the week itself was getting progressively worse.

He groaned as the doorbell rang again, knowing that with his car still parked in the driveway rather than put away in the garage, as it should be, it must be obvious to the caller that he was definitely at home.

In any other circumstances, he would have been thrilled to find Chloe standing on the doorstep, but, with the information he had so recently obtained, she was the very last person he wanted to see!

Not that she didn't look absolutely lovely, because she did, the simply designed black dress she wore a perfect foil for her long dark hair and creamy skin.

She smiled up at him. 'Are you still angry with me, or are you going to invite me in?' she prompted hopefully.

He opened the door wider so that she could come in. He wasn't in the least angry with her, hadn't been angry with her on Friday evening either. But knowing what he now knew, he wasn't sure what to say to her...

'We both look as if we're in mourning,' she said once they were in the sitting-room; Fergus was also dressed completely in black: black denims and a black shirt.

Fergus was mentally apologising to Maud for her wasted dinner, even if Chloe's visit turned out to be a short one, he felt even less like eating now.

'What can I do for you, Chloe?' he asked soberly.

She moistened her lips with the tip of her tongue, clearly not as self-possessed as she wanted to appear. 'A cup of coffee would be nice,' she suggested brightly. 'Do you mind if I sit down?'

'Help yourself,' he invited, watching brood-ingly as she did so, crossing one shapely knee over the other, her legs lightly tanned.

Stop it, Fergus, he instantly instructed him-self sternly. He was in enough of a dilemma as it was, without feeling this aching desire for Chloe.

'I wasn't actually offering you refreshment in my earlier question,' he told her dryly. 'But I'm quite happy to get you a cup of coffee.' And then she would have to go, he decided firmly as he went out to the kitchen. He had a lot of thinking to do, and he certainly couldn't do it with Chloe around!

He moved economically around the room preparing the pot of coffee, wondering why Chloe was here—wondering what on earth he could possibly find to say to her!

'I seem to have interrupted your dinner,' Chloe said apologetically from behind him. 'I didn't mean to startle you,' she continued as she saw the way he had jumped when she'd first spoken. 'Please don't let your meal get cold.' She indicated the meat pudding and veg-etables that were slowly congealing on the plate that sat on the kitchen table.

'I wasn't enjoying it anyway,' he dismissed, picking up the tray with the coffee things on. 'Let's go back into the other room, shall we?'

Chloe eyed him searchingly once they were back in the sitting-room, the coffee poured. 'Is there something wrong, Fergus?'

Everything! Almost everything. Damn it, he wished—and not for the first time—that he had never started this!

He sat down in the armchair opposite hers. 'Not particularly,' he avoided. 'Why are you here, Chloe?' He was deliberately more specific this time.

'Well...I could say I just called in to see you,' she parried. 'Or that I was just passing. Or that—'

'I believe I've already told you that I much prefer the truth to fabrication,' he cut in.

'So you did,' she returned easily. 'Maybe I should have telephoned first.' She chewed worriedly on her bottom lip.

Fergus wished she wouldn't do that! Because he would like to be the one doing it; nibbling, tasting, savouring the allure of those pouting, very kissable lips!

'You're here now,' he replied, hoping none of his inner hunger—and not for food!—showed in his expression.

She drew in a deep breath. 'Peter Ambrose has contacted my father—not officially,' she added hastily, 'concerning the proposed storyline of your book.'

Once again Fergus wished he had never even contemplated writing that particular book. Because now, in light of the new information he had received, Chloe was going to be hurt no matter what he did. Which meant she would only hate him all the more!

He sighed. 'Yes?' After his own conversation with Peter Ambrose last week, he was only surprised the other man had waited this long.

Chloe put down her coffee-cup, her hand shaking slightly. 'It isn't too late to stop all this, Fergus.' She looked across at him pleadingly.

Oh, yes, it was. Far, far too late. Because it was out of his hands now, like a tiny snowball rolling from the top of a mountain, growing bigger and bigger as it gained momentum.

He sat forward in his own chair, desperately searching for the right thing to say. 'Chloe,' he began hesitantly, 'can't you talk to your father? Perhaps try to persuade him that going back into politics is not the right thing for him to do?' Now, or ever, if Fergus's information was correct!

Her eyes widened. 'Because you want to write a book?' she questioned incredulously.

'No—'

'Don't you think you're being more than a little selfish?' she accused. 'You're a writer, you must have dozens of storylines floating around inside your head—

'I appreciate your confidence in my imaginative capabilities, Chloe,' he interrupted her. 'But I'm afraid that—'

'This is the story you want to write!' she finished, standing up agitatedly. 'Fergus, I'm pleading with you, begging, if necessary; please, please stop this.' Her eyes were full of as yet unshed tears.

He wished he could agree to do that, wished it were within his power to do so. But he had received a visit from someone this afternoon who had made that impossible...!

'Chloe, your father must have known, when he made his decision to go back into politics, that—my book apart—the past was sure to be thrown up at him again,' he tried reasoning.

'The past, yes.' She nodded. 'He's ready for that. After all, he has always maintained his innocence. But, can't you see, your book will sensationalise the whole thing? I'll do anything, Fergus,' she continued chokingly. 'Anything at all, as long as you agree not to write this book!'

Fergus felt sick, knowing that within twenty-four hours, forty-eight at the most, Chloe was going to hate him with a vengeance. And when she thought back to what she had just offered him, she was going to hate him all the more.

His gaze ran slowly up, and then equally slowly down, the slender length of her body, keeping his expression deliberately insolent even as Chloe blushed painfully. Better to hurt her now than later.

'You seem to rate your physical attributes rather highly, my dear,' he finally drawled.

Her pain obviously warred with the anger she also felt as she fought for control of her temper—and lost. 'You—'

'No more name-calling, Chloe,' Fergus advised mockingly, standing up himself now, having come to a decision during the last couple of minutes, one that required Chloe to leave. Now. 'I really don't think we have anything further to say to each other—do you?' He quirked dark brows.

Her cheeks lost all their colour at his deliberate snub. 'I can't think why I ever thought that appealing to the nice side of your nature would work—you obviously don't have one!' she exclaimed, grabbing up her car keys from the coffee-table. 'I don't know how you can sleep at night!' she finished disgustedly.

Just recently he hadn't been—and it had nothing to do with the guilty conscience Chloe was implying he should have. Just thinking of Chloe was enough to give him sleepless nights!

'As you already know, I have very little trouble doing exactly that,' he reminded her of the night she had spent in his bedroom. A night he hadn't been able to get out of his mind!

He had innocently slept that night away, completely unaware of the fact that Chloe had shared the room with him. Something he was sure, despite her recent offer, would never happen again.

'Now, if you wouldn't mind?' He glanced at his wrist-watch; only seven-thirty. He had plenty of time. He hoped! 'I have an appointment this evening.' At least, he hoped to have, after a brief telephone call.

After this visit of desperation by Chloe, he now knew he couldn't just sit here and do nothing. Even if he failed to stop that rolling snowball, he knew he had to at least try to find someone else who could. If it hadn't already crashed at the bottom of the mountain!

Chloe's mouth turned down scathingly. 'I'm sorry to have wasted your time,' she gritted through her teeth, marching over to the door.

'It was your time you were wasting,' he taunted softly.

'Obviously!' She turned briefly to glare at him, eyes sparkling deeply blue.

Fergus kept up his nonchalant pose for as long as it took Chloe to stride angrily out of the house, get into her car, and drive away. After which his shoulders slumped like a deflated balloon.

He shook his head determinedly. This wouldn't do. He had things to do. Places to go. Someone to see.

But first he had to make that telephone call...

Why was it that Fergus always made her so angry she forgot all her good intentions, all her persuasive tactics, as soon as she saw him?

And that she ended up in tears every time she left him!

Those hot rivulets of frustration and disillusionment were running down her cheeks as she drove away from his house, uncontrollable tears, as she knew she had once again failed to convince Fergus of the damage his book would do to her family.

Not only had she failed, she had totally humiliated herself by offering herself and being so callously rejected!

She would have to tell David tomorrow morning that they had no choice now; her father had to be told about what was going on. It would be so much worse if he were to learn of it from another source.

But the thought of going home, of sitting down to dinner with her parents, with that knowledge burning inside her, was not a pleasant one. Besides, after this most recent conversation with Fergus, she was positive she wouldn't be able to eat a thing...

The lights blazed welcomingly in Penny and David's house as Chloe parked her car in the driveway, and while Josh would probably have already gone to bed, eight-year-old Diana, and ten-year-old Paul would still be up. She was very fond of her niece and nephews, and at this moment their innocence seemed very appealing. Much more so than trying to get through an evening of normality with her parents!

'Hello, darling,' Penny greeted warmly as Chloe let herself into the kitchen. 'Just in time to help me bath this horror.' She ruffled the dark hair of her youngest son. 'I'm a bit behind this evening,' she cheerfully explained the fact that Josh was still up, after all. 'David had to pop out unexpectedly.'

Chloe couldn't say she exactly minded that David wasn't here; the fact that he knew what she knew, and that Penny obviously didn't, could have made her visit a little awkward.

'I would love to help with the bath,' she agreed with a smile, already feeling the tension starting to ease out of her.

Penny was such a natural mother, Chloe thought admiringly as her sister organised Diana and Paul into doing their homework before taking Josh upstairs for his bath. Her sister took responsibility for the children's car journeys to school, their horse-riding lessons, swimming, and teas with and for friends. The fact that David very often wasn't there to help her with them didn't stop her from taking it all in her stride, rarely becoming cross or impatient.

The balm of this warm and happy household was exactly what Chloe needed after her last conversation with Fergus.

'And how is the gorgeous Fergus?' Penny asked as she helped Josh undress for his bath, seeming to have picked up on at least some of Chloe's thoughts.

'He isn't,' Chloe answered with finality. 'Gorgeous, or otherwise,' she added.

Her sister showed her disappointment at this news. 'I thought he seemed rather nice.'

Chloe looked unconcerned. 'A bit too arrogant and domineering for my taste.'

'That's a shame,' Penny sympathised.

'Who's Fergus?' Josh asked guilelessly as he played with the bubbles in his bath.

Penny chuckled. 'I forgot little people have big ears,' she said apologetically to Chloe. 'He's just a friend of Aunty Chloe's, darling,' she told her youngest son as she began to shampoo his hair.

Friend hardly accurately described Fergus—at any time during their acquaintance!

'Aunty Chloe has a boyfriend,' Josh announced to his older brother and sister when they returned to the kitchen after his bath. 'His name's Fergus,' he elaborated knowingly.

And Chloe had just been thinking how adorable he looked with his hair still slightly damp, and dressed in a pair of pyjamas that sported a popular cartoon character on the front!

'Are you going to marry him, Aunty Chloe?' Diana asked excitedly; her dearest wish—and she stated it often!—was to be a bridesmaid.

Marry Fergus? She would as soon throw herself into a cage of lions! At least their attack would be swift as well as deadly...

''Fraid not, poppet,' she disappointed her niece. 'Kiss what you think is a prince nowadays and they turn into a frog!'

Diana giggled, her attention instantly diverted—as it was meant to be!—onto which bedtime story Chloe was going to read to her tonight. Diana was old enough to read to herself when she went to bed, but she occasionally liked to be indulged by having someone to read to her. And Aunty Chloe was usually only too happy to oblige.

'Is that really true?' Penny prompted half an hour later, all the children now in their bedrooms, the two women enjoying a cup of tea together in the tidy sitting-room. 'About the prince turning into a frog?' she reminded her sister laughingly as Chloe looked confused.

'I'm afraid so,' Chloe admitted. 'I think I'll just stick with my career—it's completely trustworthy, and it doesn't answer back!'

Penny made a face. 'I'm glad I'm not still out there looking for a soul mate. It seems to have become more complicated since my debutante days!' She stretched tiredly.

'Why don't you take advantage of the kids being in bed, and David's absence, and go and have a nice soak in the bath?' Chloe suggested, having seen her sister's tiredness. 'I should be getting back, anyway.' Even if the mere thought of it brought back that heavy feeling in her chest.

'I think I will.' Penny smiled in anticipation of an hour or so's relaxation. 'Thanks for helping with the kids. Give my love to Mummy and Daddy.'

Chloe didn't hurry her drive home, still not in any rush to get there. But by arriving home late she should have missed dinner, which was something; at least she wouldn't have to go through the motions of eating now, for her parents' sake.

Although her tension returned in full force, her face paling, her hands tightly grasping the steering wheel, when she reached her parents' home and saw, as well as David's blue car parked in the driveway, the now familiar dark grey sports car was also parked there.

What on earth was Fergus doing here?

As if she really needed to ask…!

Although it was now obvious to where David had been called out so unexpectedly!

It was why that concerned Chloe…

She hastily parked her own car beside Fergus's before hurrying into the house. She had left Fergus an hour and a half ago, was probably already too late to stop him doing whatever damage he had come here to do.

'Hello, darling,' her mother greeted as Chloe hurried into the sitting-room, putting down the magazine she had been flicking through to smile at her youngest daughter. 'I wondered where you had got to. Dinner has been delayed slightly, I'm afraid, your father has some sort of business meeting going on,' she explained unconcernedly.

Chloe knew exactly who that business meeting was with!

The room was empty except for her mother, which meant Fergus had to be ensconced in the study with her father and David. Discussing what? Did her father know everything now? And if he did, what would he decide to do about it?

Damn Fergus!

'Has Fergus been here long?' she enquired conversationally, resisting her first instinct—which was to march down the hallway to her father's study and demand to know exactly what Fergus thought he was doing.

'Of course, you must have seen his car in the driveway,' her mother realised. 'An hour or so. I thought at first that he had come here to see you, but he asked to see your father. You don't suppose he's formally asking for

your hand in marriage, do you?' her mother
teased mischievously. 'What fun!'

Chloe was sure that marriage, to her or anyone else, was the last thing on Fergus's mind
at the moment! Or any other moment...

'I very much doubt it,' she answered wryly.
'I see David is here too,' she ventured.

'He arrived a few minutes after Fergus,' her
mother responded. 'I must say, it's all very
mysterious.'

Not to Chloe it wasn't. Although she
couldn't say anything to her mother; she had
already been through enough over this eight
years ago.

And so the two women sat together in the
sitting-room, making light conversation, the
minutes seeming to tick by very slowly to
Chloe as she waited for the three men to
emerge from the study. It was at times like this
that she wished she did drink!

It was almost half an hour later when she
heard the men's voices out in the hallway,
breaking off her conversation with her mother
to stand up and hurry from the room.

Grim didn't even begin to describe the expressions on their faces, David leading the
way, Fergus after him, and her father following

behind; David's face was white with tension, Fergus's expression becoming arrogantly distant as he saw her standing in the hallway.

But it was her father who concerned her the most; he suddenly looked ten years older, his face grey with unhappiness, a defeated droop to his shoulders, moving with none of the energetic drive that he usually did.

Her angrily accusing gaze returned to Fergus as he drew level with her in the hallway, knowing that, for the second time in the last few days, she wanted to hit him.

'Don't say a word,' he warned, even as he reached out and took a firm hold of her upper arm. 'Walk me to my car,' he ground out.

It wasn't a request, and Chloe didn't take kindly to being ordered about by this particular man. But her efforts to release herself from his grip only succeeded in bruising her arm.

'Now,' Fergus added through gritted teeth.

Chloe shot him a fiercely angry look before turning on her heel and marching towards the front door, dragging Fergus along with her, his hold still firm on her arm.

'Well, I hope you're satisfied!' She turned on him furiously once they were outside the closed front door, glaring up at him, easily able to see him in the light over the door.

'Not particularly.' He shook his head, eyes a dull brown, his mouth a grim line.

'Then why did you do it?' Her voice broke emotionally. 'Oh, never mind—we both know why. What is my father going to do now?'

Fergus moved his shoulders slightly. 'I think you had better ask him that. Don't you?'

'I'll never forgive you for this, Fergus,' Chloe told him chokingly, fighting back the threatening tears. 'Never!'

'I didn't suppose you would,' he acknowledged dully.

'I hope your book is a complete failure,' she added childishly, knowing that it wouldn't be, that Fergus's name on it alone would make it a success. 'It deserves to be, at least!'

Fergus looked sad. 'Do any of us ever really get what we deserve?'

'You certainly should,' Chloe told him with dislike. 'I never want to see you again!'

'I didn't suppose you would,' he repeated flatly. 'But maybe one day—'

'Never,' she asserted vehemently.

'Then there's nothing more to be said, is there?' He unlocked his car. 'When you're less angry with me, and more in control where your father is concerned, I suggest you talk to him. I'm not sure how much he'll tell you. But talk to him anyway, hmm?'

Of course she would talk to her father; she didn't need Fergus McCloud to tell her what to do!

'Goodbye, Chloe,' Fergus said huskily, seeming to hesitate when it actually came to getting into his car and driving away.

'Goodbye, Fergus,' she returned crisply, feeling no such hesitation where her own feelings towards him were concerned.

She despised him utterly for the way he was intentionally, selfishly, hurting her father. Obviously writing his book meant more to him than anything else.

She hated him for treating her so callously earlier this evening, her pleadings, in light of this immediate visit to her father, so obviously meaning nothing to him.

But as he finally got into his car, reversing out the driveway before driving off, Chloe knew there was another emotion she felt towards him. Despite everything, *in* spite of everything, she knew her love for Fergus was unchanged by any of those things.

And she felt as if her heart were breaking!

CHAPTER TWELVE

'You know, laddie, as I see it there are two solutions to your problem.'

Fergus looked irritatedly across at his grandfather as the two of them enjoyed a pre-lunch whisky at Fergus's home, his grandfather having travelled down to London the previous day on one of his monthly visits. At least…his grandfather was obviously enjoying his whisky; Fergus hadn't enjoyed anything in over a week now.

'Problem?' he frowned.

His grandfather nodded, a distinguished-looking man of almost eighty, his face unlined, his body still slimly fit, only the whiteness of his hair, and the wisdom in his gaze, an indication of his age. 'You can either marry the lassie, Fergus, or forget about her. And, if you don't mind my saying so, you don't seem to be having too much luck doing the latter!'

Fergus frowned across at the elderly man. 'What lass—er, girl?' he said finally. Guardedly…

His grandfather sighed. 'As you know, I had dinner with Brice last night—'

'And my dear cousin told you about Chloe,' Fergus guessed. This was the last time he allowed Brice to even know of one of his relationships, let alone actually meet the woman in question. Although, in truth, what he had had with Chloe—briefly!—couldn't even begin to be described as a relationship.

'Chloe... Is that her name? Pretty,' his grandfather said appreciatively. 'Although nowhere near as pretty as the lassie herself, from what Brice said.' He raised questioning brows.

Pretty didn't even begin to describe Chloe...

'She's beautiful,' Fergus acknowledged dully.

'And...?' his grandfather prompted.

'And nothing!' Fergus stood up forcefully, his expression grim. 'Chloe is beautiful, charming, has a great sense of humour—'

'Married?'

'Certainly not!' Fergus snapped, glaring indignantly at his grandfather. The fact that he hadn't been too sure himself on that point initially wasn't something his grandfather needed to know. 'Although she might as well be,' he added heavily. 'She's just as out of reach!' To him, at least!

'Brice seemed under the impression she had spent the night here at least once...?' his grandfather prompted mildly.

He drew in an angry breath. 'Brice has a big mouth,' he bit out caustically.

'Actually, I think he's as worried about you as I am,' his grandfather rebuked mildly.

Fergus's family may not be as normal as Chloe's, with its parents and siblings, was, but nevertheless the three cousins and their grandfather were close, with each of them caring for the other. Fergus knew he deserved the rebuke, no matter how mildly it was given.

'There's really no need for you to be,' he reassured the old man.

Although the last ten days, since he had last seen Chloe, had been the longest Fergus had ever known. He couldn't eat, couldn't sleep, and he certainly couldn't work. All he could think about was what was Chloe doing now? Had her father spoken to her, confided in her? And if he had, how much more did Chloe hate him...?

'I think you should allow me to be the judge of that, Fergus,' his grandfather told him firmly, standing up to refill their whisky glasses. 'Tell me about her,' he said gently.

Fergus's mouth twisted wryly. 'I thought I just did.'

His grandfather shook his head impatiently. 'Who is she? What does she do? Why is she out of reach?'

Fergus knew that it was this last question that intrigued his grandfather the most—which was probably why he chose to answer the first two! 'Her name is Chloe Fox-Hamilton. She's a dress designer,' he provided economically.

'Fox-Hamilton...' his grandfather repeated slowly. 'Any relation to the politician?' His gaze had narrowed speculatively.

'Ex-politician,' Fergus corrected abruptly. 'She's his daughter,' he added defensively, aware that his grandfather probably knew about the scandal eight years ago too.

'A bad business, that,' his grandfather murmured in confirmation that he did indeed remember it. 'So she's Willie Fox-Hamilton's granddaughter, eh?' he mused interestedly.

Fergus looked at him in surprise. 'You know Chloe's grandfather?'

'I knew her father too,' his grandfather confirmed. 'Oh, not for many years now.' He smiled at Fergus's stunned expression. 'As a young boy, Paul used to accompany his father on shoots at the estate.' He frowned. 'Probably a bit before your time,' he recalled. 'I remember now that the lad dropped the double-barrelled part of his name when he went into politics. Willie Fox-Hamilton's granddaughter, aye,' he said again, this time with a definite sparkle of interest in faded blue eyes. 'If the lassie is anything like her grandfather, then I'm not surprised you're having trouble with her!'

He wasn't having trouble with her—he had just hurt her so badly she never wanted to see him again! 'I—' He broke off what he had been about to say in Chloe's defence as Maud entered the room after a brief knock, turning to look at her questioningly.

'Miss Fox-Hamilton is here to see you, Mr Fergus,' his housekeeper informed him politely.

He had left instructions with Maud last week that if Chloe should telephone, or—unbelievable as it might seem!—actually call on him in person, that, no matter what he was doing, where he was, Maud was to let him know immediately.

But he hadn't thought it would ever happen...

'Out of reach, aye, lad?' his grandfather commented dryly, looking across at him questioningly.

Fergus could feel the colour tinge his hard cheekbones. 'I—'

'Please don't bother to say you aren't at home, Fergus,' Chloe stopped him sarcastically as she walked into the room, if not unannounced, as yet uninvited, her eyes widening slightly as she saw Fergus wasn't alone. 'I hope I'm not interrupting anything?'

'Not at all, lassie,' Fergus's grandfather was the one to answer her.

Which was probably as well; Fergus was still too stunned by Chloe's unexpected appearance at his home to be able to speak!

He drank in the sight of her, his gaze narrowing, his mouth thinning, as he saw that the last ten days hadn't been kind to her, either. She had always been slender, but now she was so delicately thin she looked as if she might break, her denims very loose on her hips, the blue silk blouse looking at least a size too big. And her face, while still beautiful, had a gaunt look to it, her cheeks very pale, dark shadows beneath the deep, haunting blue of her eyes.

Fergus's own cheeks paled even more as he knew he had helped do this to her...

'In the absence of my grandson remembering his manners...' His grandfather was again the one to speak to cover the awkward silence that had fallen since Maud had quietly left the room, closing the door behind her. 'Hugh McDonald.' He held his hand out to Chloe.

'Grandson...' Chloe repeated uncomfortably even as she shook that hand, grimacing slightly as she turned to look at Fergus. 'Perhaps I should come back another time,' she said reluctantly.

'No! Er—no.' Fergus at last regained his voice, inwardly panicking at the thought of her leaving without at least having told him why she was here at all. 'I'm sure my grandfather won't mind if we delay our lunch for a short time while the two of us go through to my study and talk privately...?' He raised dark brows at his grandfather.

'Not at all,' the elderly man confirmed lightly. 'Unless Miss Fox-Hamilton would care to join us...?' He smiled enquiringly at Chloe.

'Er—no. No, thank you,' she refused awkwardly, two bright spots of colour in her cheeks now. 'I just wanted to have a few words with Fergus, and then I really must go.'

That sounded ominous, and from the too-innocent expression on his grandfather's face as he glanced across at Fergus, it was obvious that he had picked up on it too!

'Nice to have met you—Chloe, isn't it...?' his grandfather said warmly.

'Er—yes,' she confirmed, again giving Fergus a frowning look. 'Nice to have met you too, Mr McDonald.'

'Somehow I doubt that.' The elderly man chuckled wryly at her politeness. 'Would you give my regards to your father?' Hugh continued.

Fergus closed his eyes briefly as he saw the accusing look Chloe directed at him. Of all the things his grandfather could have said...

It was obvious from the anger now burning in Chloe's cheeks that she had sensed some sort of hidden sarcasm in his grandfather's words.

'Chloe...!' Fergus reached out a placating hand towards her.

'So much for classified information!' She spat the words at him scathingly, her head going back proudly. 'Well, since you seem to have told the whole world exactly what you intend doing to my family with the publication of your damned book, I see absolutely no point in us going to your study so we can talk privately!' She was breathing hard in her agitation. 'I thought you were many things, Fergus, but vindictive wasn't one of them!'

His mouth thinned at her insulting tone. 'I'm not—'

'Not vindictive?' she cut in hardly, her face animatedly beautiful in her anger. 'My father has decided to retire from public life completely and take my mother off to live in Majorca, David is to take control of all my father's business dealings here. But once the house is sold, I will no longer have a home in London to go to, so I've decided to move to Paris—'

'To Paris...?' Fergus echoed dazedly. 'When?'

'The sooner the better!' Chloe snapped. 'I just thought you might like to know! Oh, not about me,' she dismissed scornfully as Fergus still looked stunned by the things she had just told him. 'About my whole family, but my father in particular,' she bit out with distaste. 'You've won, Fergus.'

He shook his head. Chloe was leaving London. She was going to live in Paris.

'It wasn't a battle, Chloe,' he told her raggedly.

'Of course it was,' she scoffed. 'The famous Fergus McCloud versus the infamous Paul Hamilton!'

'Have you spoken to your father as I asked you to…?'

She shook her head. 'He refuses to discuss the situation. Even with my mother,' she added emotionally, her gaze hardening once again as she recognised that emotion. 'He's made his decision. And that's the way it's going to be.'

The way it shouldn't be, Fergus knew frustratedly. But what else could he have done? What could he do now? What could he have done ten days ago, when he'd discovered the truth, that would put the situation right? Even if he told Chloe that truth, in the face of Paul Hamilton's intransigence it would solve nothing. And her family, though it was already shattered enough, was slowly unravelling.

'There, Fergus.' She gave a humourless smile. 'I've told you what you must have been burning to know, so now I can leave.' She turned sharply on her heel and did exactly that.

'Well, don't just stand there like a great gork, laddie,' his grandfather rasped. 'Go after her!'

And do what? Say what? He had made an agreement with Paul Hamilton ten days ago, an agreement that meant, without the other man's permission, he couldn't tell Chloe anything—and the other man flatly refused to give that permission.

'She's Willie Fox-Hamilton's granddaughter, all right,' Hugh opined appreciatively. 'And Brice was quite right, she is beautiful. If I were forty years younger I'd go after her myself—'

'Well, you're not!' Fergus retorted furiously, fighting an inner battle with himself.

He wanted to go after Chloe, of course he did. But he knew, as he had known ten days ago, that ultimately he could change nothing. Paul Hamilton, in making his decision to move to Majorca, had obviously made his choice. It was a choice that only Paul had the right to make...

'Are ye a man or a wee mousie, laddie?' His grandfather's Scottish accent became more pronounced with his increasing anger at Fergus's lack of response. 'Or is it that you're what the lassie just said you were...?' He looked at Fergus disapprovingly.

Fergus's gaze blazed across the room at the elderly man. 'Grandfather, don't interfere in something you know absolutely nothing about!' he snapped coldly.

His grandfather's gaze flashed back the same angry message. 'I admit I have absolutely no idea what all that was about just now, but what I do know is I wouldn't let a lassie like Chloe walk out of my house, my life, in the state that wee lassie just did!' he challenged.

Chloe wasn't just walking out of his house, his life, she was leaving England too. To go and live in Paris. The home of fashion. Soon to be Chloe's home, too...

Chloe was shaking so badly when she left the house that for a few moments she didn't even have the strength to walk the short distance to her car. Instead she leant weakly against the wall outside, willing the world to stop tilting on a dangerous angle.

She had needed to see Fergus one last time, needed—never mind what she needed! It had been a mistake. The last of many she had made where Fergus McCloud was concerned.

'Chloe…!' Suddenly Fergus was standing there beside her, his hand like a vice about the top of her arm. 'Please don't cry, Chloe!' he pleaded raggedly.

She instantly blinked back the tears she hadn't even realised were falling. 'I'm not crying. I—I have an insect in my eye,' she excused lamely.

She had done nothing *but* cry the last ten days, her emotions towards Fergus see-sawing drastically between anger and despair. On the one hand she was so angry with him she wanted to spit at him, and on the other she loved him so much she just wanted to launch herself into his arms and beg him to put everything back as it had been before she'd known about the book he intended writing. But at the same time still keeping Fergus in her life…

'Let's go for a walk,' he muttered grimly, that vice-like grip remaining on her arm as he turned her towards the park gates across the road from his house.

Of course, they couldn't go back into his house, Chloe realised numbly; his grandfather was there. What on earth must Hugh McDonald think of her outburst just now?

Not that it really mattered; she doubted she would ever see the elderly man again!

'Let's sit here,' Fergus suggested as they reached a park bench that faced towards a pond.

Chloe sat, glad to feel the support of the bench beneath her, her legs feeling slightly shaky now. But she didn't remember when she had last eaten, let alone slept, so was it any wonder she felt so awful?

It was so peaceful sitting here, the sound of traffic outside the park muted by the trees and bushes that surrounded them, couples walking along together arm in arm, mothers with young children feeding the ducks that glided so smoothly over the surface of the pond.

Hard to believe, when surrounded by such serene normality, that her own world was falling apart!

Fergus sat grimly at her side, leaning forward on the bench, the atmosphere in the park not seeming to be having the same calming influence on him.

Chloe studied him surreptitiously from beneath lowered lashes. He looked so good to her, so tall and strong, so sure of himself, so—so Fergus!

He shook his head. 'I don't know what to say, Chloe.'

Her mouth quirked. 'There doesn't seem to be a lot either of us can say,' she replied dully.

Fergus turned to look at her where she sat back on the bench. 'No—I mean, I really don't know what to say to you. There's so much I could say, but—damn it!' he exclaimed angrily. 'I can't!'

Chloe sighed heavily. 'Don't worry about it, Fergus—'

'Of course I worry about it!' he snapped, his hands clenched into fists. 'You look bloody awful,' he rasped frustratedly.

'Thanks!'

'I'm only stating a fact, Chloe,' he carried on. 'Can't your father and mother see what this is doing to you?'

'I think they have other things on their minds other than how I look.'

Her father was grimly going through the process of preparing his business affairs for David to take over, as well as putting the house up for sale, in preparation for the move to Majorca. Her mother was trying to remain cheerful, outwardly at least, by calmly going through the process of supporting him in his decision.

It was all like a nightmare to Chloe!

Fergus shook his head. 'Then they damn well shouldn't have! You're their daughter, too, and— Your father is really going to just up stakes and move to Majorca?' he queried disbelievingly.

Chloe nodded. 'We have a villa there. He's just decided it's the right time for him to retire.'

'Rubbish!' Fergus cried. 'It's time for him to fight damn it.'

Chloe eyed him humorously. 'Do you always swear this much when you're angry or upset?'

'Angry *and* upset,' he corrected. 'And damn is pretty mild considering how deeply I'm feeling both those emotions at the moment!'

Chloe had no idea why he should be feeling either, and, in truth, she felt too weary to find out why.

'Damn is Darcy's favourite swear word,' Fergus mused distractedly.

'She's your cousin Logan's wife,' Chloe remembered, wondering what significance the other woman had on this conversation, knowing that she probably didn't, that it was simply a case of she and Fergus having nothing else to say to each other! 'Are they back from their honeymoon now?'

'Last weekend,' he confirmed. 'And they're obviously idyllically happy,' he added sardonically.

Fergus obviously still hadn't quite got over his feelings of loss where his cousin was concerned...

He looked at his feet. 'I never meant to hurt anyone, you know, Chloe.'

She put a consoling hand on his arm. 'If Logan and Darcy are that happy together I doubt they've even noticed you aren't exactly over the moon at their marriage,' she assured him.

Fergus turned to her. 'I'm not talking about Logan and Darcy,' he dismissed impatiently. 'I'm over that stupidity, have been for weeks. I was referring to your family when I said I never meant to hurt anyone,' he corrected harshly.

She sighed. 'It was always a time bomb waiting to go off.' She had accepted that much herself now. With the Susan Stirling situation unsolved, any move her father made politically was always bound to cause a certain amount of controversy.

What was happening now, her parents' move to Majorca, the breaking-up of the family home, while not being exactly pleasant, had perhaps always been inevitable. She had come to that much of a conclusion over the last ten days!

Fergus turned to her fully, his gaze intense as he looked at her. 'I tried to tell you earlier— when you thought I was going to deny being vindictive. I've decided not to write the book, after all.'

Chloe's eyes widened. 'Why ever not?'

His gaze no longer met hers. 'I—My heart is no longer in it. Besides, as you said...' his mouth twisted self-derisively '...I'm a writer, I have a lot of other plot-lines in my head that I can use, without hurting anyone in the process.'

Now he decided not to write the book, now—when it could do no good whatsoever. The damage had already been done, and for Chloe and her family nothing was ever going to be the same again.

'I'm glad, Fergus.' She squeezed his arm in gratitude before removing her hand. Although she could still feel the strength of him beneath her fingertips, the aching need to— No! It was over. All of it was over. 'Would you please pass on my apologies to your grandfather for my behaviour just now? He must think I'm incredibly rude!'

Fergus gave the ghost of a smile. 'Actually his last comment to me was if he were forty years younger he would be chasing after you himself!'

'Did he?' Chloe smiled herself now, even if it was tinged with sadness. Fergus would never chase after her...

'He did,' Fergus responded. 'You really are going to live in Paris?'

'I really am,' Chloe confirmed lightly. 'I made a lot of contacts when I lived there for a year, and now that I've established my own label... I've had the offer of doing a collection for next spring. Now seems as good a time as any to take up that offer,' she added ruefully.

It hadn't been an easy decision to make, but, with all that was going on around her, Chloe had decided this was probably a good time for her to set up her own household. And Paris was a good place for her to make a start.

Besides, if she were in Paris, intensely involved with her work, she might just be able to put Fergus from her mind for more than a few minutes at a time!

'How long do you intend staying there?' Fergus asked huskily.

She had no idea; all she could think about at the moment was getting away from England. From Fergus...

'I may decide to stay permanently,' she replied.

'Permanently!' he echoed incredulously.

'I told you there will be no family home here for me to come back to. Oh, no doubt I'll come back from time to time to visit Penny, David, and the children. But other than that I'll have no reason to come back.' No reason at all, except the man she loved lived here... 'If you're ever in Paris, why don't you look me up?' she felt compelled to add, unable to bear the thought of never seeing Fergus again. 'I'll be in the phone book.'

'Under Fox or Hamilton?' he rejoined gruffly.

She smiled sheepishly at his unmistakable reference to her initial subterfuge as regards her name. How long ago had that been now? Three weeks? Four? It seemed like a lifetime ago, so much had happened.

'Both,' she answered him firmly. 'Keep an eye out for the Foxy label, too, Fergus; I intend to make it one of the most well known in women's fashion!'

He gave her a considering look. 'I think you'll probably do just that,' he said.

'I hope so!' She stood up decisively. 'Now, I think I've kept you from your grandfather, and delayed your lunch together, quite long enough,' she announced briskly.

Fergus stood up more slowly. 'I can't believe your father is just giving up like this—'

'He isn't giving up!' Chloe defended angrily, her earlier calm completely erased. 'Someone held a loaded gun up to his head— he's just trying to move out of the way before they pull the trigger!'

'You mean me?' Fergus queried.

'Of course I mean you!' she confirmed impatiently. 'Who else could it have been?'

'But-I'm-not-writing-the-book!' he enunciated clearly.

'This time.' Chloe steadily met his gaze.

His expression darkened. 'At any time!'

She shrugged. 'You'll have to take that up with my father. But I don't think it will make any difference. His mind seems to be pretty well made up.'

'Then it will just have to be unmade,' Fergus ground out through his teeth.

'It's too late, Fergus,' she told him huskily.

She had known she had to see Fergus this one last time. Not through any wish to try to put things right; she knew it was too late for that. But she had just needed to see him, to commit his face, the way he talked, the way he moved, to memory. But other than that, it was as she had said: too late...

'We'll see about that,' Fergus said grimly.

'Just leave it, Fergus.' She put a beseeching hand on his arm. 'Before anyone else gets hurt.'

He gave her a sharply searching look, before looking quickly away again. 'I'll call you—if I'm ever in Paris.'

She looked at him for several minutes, knowing that this really was goodbye. After all the times she had told him she never wanted to see him again, he was now the one saying goodbye to her...!

'Do that,' she finally said before turning to slowly walk away, knowing that her heart really was breaking.

CHAPTER THIRTEEN

'WELL, laddie, it seems to me you've got yourself into a merry old tangle,' Fergus's grandfather pronounced. The two of them were lin-
gering over brandies after their meal. A meal
Fergus had neither eaten nor enjoyed.

'I can assure you, there's nothing merry
about it,' Fergus answered dully.

He had returned to the house, eventually,
more out of consideration for his grandfather
than a real wish to be here. Over lunch the
elderly man had dragged the whole sorry story
from him.

Fergus couldn't say he wasn't glad to share
it with someone, but his grandfather's condem-
nation was all he needed on top of his own
feelings of guilt.

'And you say Chloe has no idea of the
truth?' His grandfather looked serious.

'None,' Fergus confirmed heavily. 'And before you say it—I have no intention of telling
her what really happened, either!' He looked
at his grandfather unblinkingly. 'I made a

promise to Paul Hamilton over a week ago that the truth would go no further than the four walls of his study.'

'You've just told me, laddie,' his grandfather pointed out dryly.

'Only in the terms of a confessional,' Fergus maintained; he and his two cousins had always been able to talk to their grandfather when they hadn't been able to confide in anyone else, especially parents, knowing that what they told him would go no further.

'So you intend keeping this promise to Paul Hamilton,' his grandfather realised impatiently. 'I know I brought you all up, you, Logan and Brice—despite the men your mothers may have married!—to be McDonalds. Men of your word. But there's a time and a place for it—and this is neither the time nor the place!'

Fergus shook his head. 'I disagree—I think this is exactly the time and the place.' Even though it meant he was losing Chloe.

Not that she had ever been his to lose...

But without this tangled mess, without his proposed book, without her father, without— There were too many withouts, he realised heavily. Chloe had never been his, and now she never would be.

'And what about Chloe?' his grandfather persisted.

'You heard her as well as I did, Grandfather; she's going to live in Paris,' Fergus muttered before taking a large swallow from his glass of brandy.

'And you're just going to let her do that?' the older man queried.

'I'm just going to let her do that,' Fergus confirmed.

His grandfather sighed frustratedly. 'I admit I brought you all up to be men of your word, but I didn't think I had brought any of you up to be idiots as well!'

Fergus's smile lacked humour. 'Chloe would not thank me for telling her the truth.' It certainly wouldn't bring her running into his arms!

So much for his claim 'the truth shall make you free'; in his particular case, the truth had put him in a prison. A prison of silence...

'Don't you think she should be the one to be the judge of that?' his grandfather asked.

'Probably,' he conceded. 'But I don't have the right to—'

'The way I see it, you have every right,' the older man cut in.

Fergus raised dark brows. 'And just how do you work that out, Grandfather?'

'Because you love her!' the elderly man told him.

Fergus sat back abruptly, staring across at his grandfather in stunned disbelief.

Did he love Chloe?

The ache in his chest, the black bottomless void that had appeared in his life at the mere thought of her move to Paris, seemed to say that he did…

Fergus stood up abruptly, walking over to the window, staring slightlessly outside.

He loved Chloe…

He *loved* Chloe…?

He loved *Chloe*!

How long had he been in love with her? He didn't know. But he did love her. Was in love with her. Loved everything about her, from the top of her beautiful head to the end of her delicate toes. He even loved the temper she had displayed from time to time!

But, most of all, he loved the loyalty she had shown to her father, in the past, but especially these last few weeks. Her herculean efforts on the other man's behalf to ensure that no book was written that could upset her father's return to politics. The way she maintained her father's innocence even in the face of her father's own refusal to defend himself.

What wouldn't he give to have Chloe love him in that same, unquestioning, all-forgiving way!

'Well, Fergus?' his grandfather prompted softly from across the dining-room.

Fergus drew in a deeply controlling breath before turning to face the other man. 'Well, what?' His manner was deliberately obtuse. 'This isn't a fairy tale, Grandfather, this is real life, and in real life the prince doesn't always get the princess!'

'Not when he's a pigheaded idiot, he doesn't, no!' his grandfather conceded disgustedly, standing up himself now. 'I can see that there's no reasoning with you, lad, so if you'll excuse me? I promised Darcy and Logan I would go over and see them this afternoon.'

In truth, Fergus was glad of the respite, needed time with his own thoughts. If only to come to terms with loving Chloe!

Strange, but he had never thought he would ever fall in love. Not that he had deliberately set out not to; his parents' divorce, and his subsequent move to Scotland to live with his grandfather, hadn't put him off falling in love. In fact, his childhood and teenage years in Scotland couldn't have been more idyllic! It was just, as the years had passed, with only brief relationships in his life, and none of them based on love, he had thought it would never happen to him.

But now it had. And with Chloe Fox-Hamilton, of all women. The one woman who had every reason to hate him.

He was under no illusions. While he didn't agree that he had held a loaded gun to Paul Hamilton's head, he did realise he had been the catalyst to all that had happened the last three weeks.

But that was something, he knew, Chloe could never forgive him for...

Perhaps in time—?

No, he accepted. Time wouldn't take away the sting of the destruction he had unwittingly caused in her father's life—as well as her own!

But what was his own life going to be like, loving Chloe, and knowing she would never be his?

He had to try, one last time, to speak to Paul Hamilton, to make the other man see reason, to ask him once again to fight this thing. He had to!

Because Fergus really wasn't sure he could live the rest of his life knowing he loved Chloe but could never tell her so...!

Mrs Hamilton answered his call herself. Fergus would recognise that politely honed voice anywhere—it was just like Chloe's, only more mature.

'I'm afraid Paul is in a business meeting at the moment, Mr McCloud,' Diana said apologetically once Fergus had introduced himself and asked to speak to the other man. 'He seems to do nothing else at the moment,' she added wistfully. 'Could I get him to call you— Just a moment, Mr McCloud, I think I hear my husband now,' she said briskly, silence at her end of the line for several moments.

Fergus tapped his fingers impatiently on the desktop in front of him as he waited for Diana to come back on the line. Perhaps he shouldn't have bothered to telephone first. Perhaps he should have just gone over to the house—because there was always the possibility that Paul would refuse to see him.

But there had always been the chance that, having gone to the house completely unexpectedly, he might have accidentally bumped into Chloe. And, after lunchtime, he wasn't sure either of them were up to that!

'Sorry about that, Mr McCloud,' Diana came back on the line. 'My husband wonders if you would care to join us for dinner this evening?'

Fergus was stunned by the invitation. Not that he and Paul Hamilton had parted on bad terms, but he certainly hadn't expected the other man would ever want to sit down to dinner with him again!

'It's by way of being a farewell dinner,' Diana continued at his silence. 'One of several we're giving to say goodbye to family and friends. You see, Paul and I are moving to Majorca next month.'

He already knew that. But obviously, from her warm tone, Diana still had no idea of his own part in the necessity for their move...

Dinner with family and friends was not exactly what he had had in mind when it came to talking to Paul Hamilton again. But it did have the advantage of his being able to see Chloe again. And maybe, just maybe, the fact that her parents had invited him to dinner might help her to see that they at least held no grudge against him...

'I would like that very much, thank you,' he accepted; his grandfather would just have to forgive him for being a less than attentive host!

'Eight for eight-thirty, then,' Diana told him lightly before ringing off.

Fergus slowly put down his own receiver. The decision made, he was now full of indecision, totally unsure how Chloe would react to his being a dinner guest of her parents this evening.

The two of them had said goodbye earlier today, and he had no reason to feel she would be in the least pleased to see him again, as a dinner guest of her parents, or otherwise.

But maybe he was just worrying unnecessarily.

Maybe Chloe wouldn't even be there this evening!

Chloe was not looking forward to the dinner party tonight. Oh, she realised that her parents felt a need to say goodbye to friends before their permanent move to Majorca, but wouldn't it have been better to have just thrown one big party and got it over with in one go, rather than a series of small dinner parties like the one this evening?

Obviously her parents didn't think so, had decided they could cope with their parting if it were done in small stages. Chloe was willing to support them in whatever they decided to do. Which was why, even though a dinner party was the last thing she felt in the mood for, she was determined to be there for them.

Penny and David, showing the same family loyalty, were already downstairs when Chloe entered the sitting-room shortly before eight o'clock. Penny looked pale, but seemed as determined as Chloe to make all this as pleasant for their parents as possible.

Chloe was a little surprised when, shortly after eight o'clock, the first of the dinner guests were shown in. Peter and Jean Ambrose! She had known there were to be eight of them sitting down to dinner, but had no idea who the four guests were to be.

Obviously this particular dinner party was going to be worse than she had imagined it would be. She knew that her father hadn't yet informed the Leader of the Opposition of his decision to quit not only politics but Britain too; obviously all that was going to change to-night.

Chloe winced in her sister's direction, Penny giving a heavy shake of her head before she turned to look over to where their parents were now greeting the other couple.

Their father looked so handsome in the black evening clothes, their mother as lovely as ever in a dress Chloe had designed for her, its style fitted, the blue the same colour as Diana's eyes.

'Mr McCloud,' the butler announced a few minutes later.

Chloe gasped, her hand tightened around her glass of mineral water, her face draining of all colour as she saw that it was indeed Fergus who now entered the room. Fergus as she re-membered him from that first night: arrogantly self-assured, tall, and very handsome in his evening clothes.

What was he doing here? He hadn't men-tioned he was dining with her parents when she'd seen him earlier today. What—?

'And Mr McDonald,' the butler announced before Chloe had even had a chance to recover from her first shock of the evening.

Her gaze moved sharply from Fergus to the doorway behind him. Hugh McDonald, Fergus's grandfather, stood there. And any idea Chloe might have had that his call was unexpected was instantly dispelled as she took in his distinguished appearance in black evening suit and snowy white shirt.

It was bad enough that Fergus was here, but what on earth was his grandfather doing here, too?

Perhaps, as his grandfather was obviously staying with Fergus at the moment, that was why he'd been invited too. She was sure Fergus would have had no difficulty in finding a female partner for the evening if he had wanted one!

She turned accusing eyes on Fergus, only to see that he looked as stunned by Hugh McDonald's appearance as she felt; he *hadn't* known his grandfather was going to be here, either.

He didn't look pleased to see him!

Chloe strolled over to where the two men, having said their hellos to her parents, were

now in a muted, but obviously heated, conversation.

'—for visiting Darcy and Logan today! I
don't know what you're up to, Grandfather,'
Fergus was telling the older man angrily as
Chloe approached them. 'But it had better not
have anything to do with our conversation this
afternoon.'

Hugh McDonald looked completely unperturbed by his grandson's less than welcoming
behaviour, turning to smile at Chloe as she
joined them. 'May I say, my dear, you look
absolutely stunning this evening,' he told her
admiringly. 'I did tell you I knew your father,'
he added, his eyes twinkling mischievously.

'So you did,' she replied. 'And thank you,'
Chloe accepted the compliment, her dress a
soft, muted gold, above-knee length, sleeve-
less, and with a scooped neckline that showed
the creamy swell of her breasts. 'You're looking rather distinguished yourself,' she returned
the compliment with a lightness she was far
from feeling.

What on earth were Fergus and his grandfather doing here? Hugh McDonald had given
every impression earlier today that he was ac-
quainted with her father, although Chloe could

never remember meeting him before. And as for Fergus—! She would have thought he was the last person her father would want to see just now!

The elderly man grinned at her roguishly. 'The McDonald men have always aged well.' He looked pointedly at Fergus.

A grim-faced Fergus, who hadn't so much as looked at her yet, let alone spoken to her!

'But Fergus is a McCloud,' she returned with saccharine sweetness, turning to look challengingly at Fergus.

He finally returned her gaze, mockery in those dark brown eyes. 'As my grandfather would no doubt be only too happy to tell you, I'm a McCloud in name only!'

Despite their argument a few minutes ago, there was obviously a deep affection between the two men. In fact, they were more like father and son.

'Come and meet my sister and her husband,' she suggested lightly to Hugh McDonald as she draped her arm through his. 'You too, Fergus, if you would like to?' She arched dark brows at him.

'I've already met them, thanks,' he said dismissively. 'I think I'll just go and get reacquainted with Peter Ambrose instead.' He turned sharply on his heel to stroll across the room and join Peter Ambrose and his wife.

Hugh McDonald chuckled as he stood beside Chloe. 'You'll have to excuse Fergus, I'm afraid, my dear.' He gave a rueful shake of his silvery head. 'He never was any good at sharing the things that matter to him,' he added enigmatically.

At least, it was enigmatic to Chloe; she had absolutely no idea what Hugh McDonald was talking about. What she did know was that Fergus was behaving extremely rudely this evening. More so than usual!

'Come and say hello to Penny and David,' she invited again, smoothly making the introductions seconds later, slightly relieved when David took the lead in the conversation with the older man, having apparently spent a lot of his school holidays as a child fishing in different parts of Scotland.

The respite gave Chloe chance to look at Fergus unobserved. He was chatting quite naturally with Peter and Jean Ambrose and her parents, showing none of the bad-tempered rudeness of a few minutes ago. She didn't think she would ever be able to fathom out exactly what Fergus—

She wouldn't have chance to fathom out the workings of Fergus McCloud's mind! She would shortly be moving to Paris, and Fergus, well, who knew what—or who!—Fergus would be moving on to?

At least...she had thought she was unobserved in looking longingly at Fergus!

Hugh McDonald, while smoothly keeping up his conversation with David, was actually looking at her, one silver brow raised in mute enquiry.

Chloe felt her cheeks colour with embarrassment as she hastily looked away from that searching gaze.

Not that she fared any better at dinner; for reasons best known to herself, her mother had seated Chloe between Fergus and his grandfather! Hugh McDonald was charming enough, but Fergus barely spoke a word to her.

In fact, apart from the elderly Scot, who kept the conversation flowing, everyone else at the table seemed as subdued as Chloe.

'How do you think the general election will go next year?' Hugh McDonald addressed his remark, quite naturally, to the Leader of the Opposition.

'I—' Peter broke off his reply to look at Penny, who had just dropped her knife on the floor, the eight of them having reached the main course of their meal.

'Sorry,' Penny muttered before bending to pick up the knife.

Chloe shot her sister a sympathetic grimace as she straightened; obviously the strain of the evening was getting to her too. Which wasn't surprising. Penny was as aware as she was that their father hadn't yet spoken to Peter Ambrose about his future political plans—or lack of them.

'You were saying?' Hugh McDonald prompted Peter Ambrose.

'Since when have you been interested in English politics, Grandfather?' Fergus cut in hardly, the darkness of his eyes, to Chloe's frowning gaze, seeming to flash a warning to the older man.

Hugh grinned wolfishly. 'Since they started leaving us alone to run our own country!' he answered controversially.

Peter Ambrose chuckled. 'A Scotsman through and through, eh?'

'It's the most beautiful place on God's green earth,' Hugh McDonald confirmed decisively. 'So, what are your predictions for the next election?'

Peter smiled. 'We're going to win, of course.'

'Of course.' Hugh chuckled. 'And what post do you have in mind in your future government for our friend here?' He looked across at Chloe's father admiringly.

Peter Ambrose looked taken aback by the directness of the question.

As well he might. Not too many people had actually been aware of the fact that Chloe's father was contemplating going back into the political arena. And even fewer people knew he had since decided not to!

She looked at Hugh McDonald with shrewd eyes. Just how much did he know about this situation!? Whatever he knew, it didn't take two guesses to know exactly who it was who had told him!

Chloe turned accusing eyes on Fergus, his shrug of resignation telling her that he had no more hope than she did of diverting his grandfather from this potentially explosive conversation.

'Do something,' she ground out in a hushed voice.

'Other than tying him up and gagging him, you mean?' Fergus returned as angrily.

'Just gagging him will do,' she whispered, her eyes flashing deeply blue.

Fergus gave an impatient sigh. 'I—'

'What are you two lovebirds whispering about so cosily?' his grandfather enquired teasingly.

Fergus's expression was grim as he looked across Chloe to his grandfather. 'Hardly lovebirds, Grandfather,' he dismissed icily. 'And could it not just be that we find politics dull table conversation?'

Chloe gasped at the comment, knowing that Fergus, while trying to defuse this potentially dangerous conversation, had probably just insulted half the people seated at the table as a consequence!

Silver brows rose over shrewd blue eyes. 'I find that hard to believe in Chloe's case,' Hugh returned. 'I'm sure she's as eager as we all are to see her father returned to his rightful place in the political arena.'

'You see, Paul, I told you you've been worrying far too much about what people will have to say at your return.' Peter Ambrose smiled his approval of Hugh McDonald's remark. 'People do have very short memories.'

'But selective ones,' Chloe's father replied, his face now white with strain. 'And, in view of that—'

'No, Daddy, I can't let you do this!'

Chloe looked across at Penny in stunned surprise at her sudden outburst. Her sister had been unusually subdued all evening, but now she looked positively ill, her face grey, her eyes swimming with tears as she stood up to face them all.

'I've kept quiet until now, Daddy,' Penny spoke directly to their father now. 'I've tried to respect the decision you made eight years ago,' she continued emotionally. 'But I can't let you make any more sacrifices on my behalf.'

Their mother reached out a soothing hand towards her. 'Penny, darling—'

'Or you either, Mummy.' Penny shook her head decisively. 'Or Chloe,' she added enigmatically before taking in a shaky breath and looking around the dining-table at them all. 'It's time the truth was told. All of it.' She was looking at David now. 'Isn't it...?' she prompted him.

Chloe had absolutely no idea what was going on. But as she looked around the table, at her parents, the Ambroses, Hugh McDonald, Fergus, all their expressions full of sympathy, rather than her own puzzlement, as they looked at Penny, Chloe knew that she was the only one here who didn't...

And for the first time she also became aware that Fergus was tightly gripping one of her hands in his!

CHAPTER FOURTEEN

FERGUS tightened his grip on Chloe's hand as he sensed she was about to remove it.

This situation had arisen so quickly it had spiralled out of his control. If he could do nothing else for Chloe, he could at least be here for her. Even if she didn't want him to be!

'David?' Penny pressed her husband again, her expression full of tenderness, but at the same time resigned.

Fergus couldn't help wishing it hadn't come to this, and he shot his grandfather a reproving look, knowing that in this case Hugh *had* been the catalyst to this situation. He had obviously decided to take matters into his own hands this afternoon, the visit to Logan just a ruse—and, dearly as Fergus had always loved and admired his grandfather, at this particular moment he felt like strangling him!

Paul Hamilton stood up. 'I really don't want you to do this, Penny.' He crossed to his eldest daughter's side. 'There's really no need, darling,' he assured her as he took her in his arms.

Penny gazed at him unflinchingly, almost the same height as her father in her high-heeled shoes. 'David and I discussed it before coming out this evening, Daddy,' she said softly. 'We've decided, for everyone's sake, that it would be better if we just made a clean sweep of things.' She looked at the other dinner guests. 'And, as everyone with any relevance to this situation is here this evening—'

'I don't think my grandfather and I come under that category,' Fergus interjected.

Chloe, he noted achingly, still looked totally bewildered. In a few moments she was going to be well and truly stunned; he had been more than a little thrown by the truth himself!

Penny gave him a wistful smile. 'Oh, I think you do, Fergus,' she said knowingly. 'And as for your grandfather—he was the one who helped me to see this afternoon when he came to see me that this madness had to stop, that, painful as the truth might be, it has to be better than pushing it to the back of my mind and hoping the thing will just go away!' Her voice broke emotionally over those last words.

'Penny...!' David was instantly on his feet, crossing to his wife's side to take her hand in his. 'Don't do this to yourself,' he pleaded gruffly. 'I'm the one who was to blame—'

'Nonsense,' Penny put in strongly. 'If I hadn't had an affair—'

'Your husband is right, Penny,' Fergus's grandfather was—surprisingly—the one to interrupt this time. 'You have no need to do this. Everyone here—with the exception of Chloe...' he turned to smile at her apologetically '...is aware of what happened eight years ago. There's no need to keep beating yourself with the same stick,' he told Penny gently. 'You and David had a few problems eight years ago, they unfortunately, ultimately, with Peter's agreement, led to your father's resignation from politics. It's only the last factor that is of any importance now,' he assured her firmly.

Fergus could feel Chloe's tension as she sat at his side, her hand tightly gripping his now. Although Fergus was sure she was completely unaware of how tightly she was clinging to him; she would never willingly have shown such shocked dismay—to anyone!—as the truth finally dawned on her.

Because David Latham, Penny's husband, Chloe's brother-in-law, had been Susan Stirling's lover eight years ago...

Fergus had been stunned himself ten days ago when David Latham had come to see him, admitting the true circumstances to him, adding that he had decided to go to the press himself and tell them everything, no matter what the personal cost might be, as a way of clearing Paul of any wrongdoing eight years ago.

This was the snowball running down the hill, getting bigger and bigger, and totally out of control!

Paul had known exactly what had taken place eight years ago, had discussed it with Peter Ambrose, and taken the blame to save his eldest daughter any more unhappiness.

Eight years ago David and Penny had been going through a difficult time in their marriage. Penny had admitted to David that she had briefly, stupidly, become involved with another man. David had gone—again very briefly—off the rails himself at the admission.

As well he might, Fergus had inwardly acknowledged. In the same circumstances, Fergus knew he was capable of doing the same. That any man was.

Unfortunately, David's brief affair with Susan Stirling had resulted in the other woman, once he had ended the affair, becoming totally obsessed with him. She'd followed him everywhere, telephoned him at home, threatened to tell Penny about them.

By this time David and Penny had managed to work out their problems, had had a second child on the way, and David had known Susan Stirling couldn't be allowed to do that, had told her that their affair was definitely over, that he would never leave Penny, that he loved his wife. That was when Susan Stirling had told him she was expecting their child.

'You knew about this!' Chloe turned accusingly to Fergus now.

He swallowed hard, knowing she had a right to be angry with him. But what else could he have done ten days ago but respect David Latham's confidence?

After thinking about David's confession for a while, and following on from Chloe's visit to him that same day, he had actually managed to put a stop to the other man going to the press with the story, by going to see Paul Hamilton and telling him of the younger man's intention. But he had done so at the price of

promised silence on his own part. To everyone. And that included Chloe.

'Yes, I knew,' he confirmed quietly.

Chloe snorted. 'All this time…!'

In real time, ten days wasn't so long. But to
Fergus it seemed more like a lifetime he had
been keeping the truth from Chloe. And he
could see by the accusation in her face that it
had seemed much longer to Chloe too.

'Your father acted in good faith eight years
ago, did what he had to to protect his eldest
daughter, her husband, and their children from
the publicity that would have ensued if the
truth were known. In the circumstances, would
you have expected me to do any less?' He
looked at her searchingly.

She snatched her hand away from his before
standing up. 'You should have told me, Pen,'
she told her older sister gently as she moved
to her side. 'I'm not a child, you know,' she
rebuked.

Penny reached out to grasp her hand. 'Eight
years ago you were,' she reasoned. 'Besides, I
had to respect Daddy's judgement, after all
that he had done for us.' She looked lovingly
at the man who had sacrificed so much for her
sake eight years ago.

'I would do it all again,' Paul assured her gruffly.

'But don't you see, man, there's no need for anyone to make any more sacrifices?' Fergus's grandfather was the one to cut impatiently into the conversation. 'What really happened eight years ago is only relevant to six people in this room—for the moment I'm excluding Fergus and myself,' he added with an apologetic glance in Fergus's direction.

A glance Fergus acknowledged with a rueful shake of his head; his grandfather never had been able to resist playing God occasionally. But in this particular case he seemed to have excelled himself!

'Five of you have always known the truth.' Hugh included the Leader of the Opposition and his wife in his glance now. 'And it's provided no barrier to Paul's decision to re-enter politics. What I'm really trying to say, Paul—'

'And, as usual, taking his time about it,' Fergus couldn't resist putting in dryly.

His grandfather shot him a dark glance. 'As it appears to be your proposed book that started all this, laddie, I would keep quiet if I were you!'

Fergus gave a smile of acceptance at his grandfather's words. There was no doubting it had been the synopsis of his next book that had set this particular snowball in motion. 'For the last time,' he grated, standing up impatiently himself now, 'I am not writing the damned book!'

'Exactly,' Hugh confirmed with satisfaction. 'So, effectively, apart from the odd negative comment, there will be no recurrence of the publicity you received eight years ago. And as such, there will be no barrier to your going back into politics, Paul. Because at this point in time, nothing has actually changed from when you initially made your decision several months ago.' He turned triumphantly to the other man.

Fergus wasn't absolutely sure he agreed with that last sentiment; Chloe's feelings towards him had definitely changed. She hadn't been over-enamoured of him before tonight, but a few minutes ago she had looked at him with open loathing!

'Peter has always known the truth,' Hugh continued, 'and he wants you back in his future government. Your wife, eldest daughter, and her husband have always known the truth too. As I see it, it's only Chloe who has to reassess her way of thinking. Isn't it, my dear...?' he prompted gently.

Fergus looked at Chloe too, his heart aching at the paleness of her face, her eyes deeply blue with inner pain.

'Reassess her way of thinking...'

At the moment, she couldn't think at all, felt as if she had been hit over the head with a sledgehammer!

Oh, she had always known her father wasn't guilty of what he had been accused eight years ago, had never wavered in that opinion for even a moment. But that it could have been David who had been Susan Stirling's lover had never even occurred to her...

However, these things happened in marriages sometimes, people did make mistakes, and she had no doubt that her sister and David were extremely happy together now, and had been so for many years, that the two of them loved each other deeply, as they did their children.

One thing was very clear to her, however...

'Mr McDonald is right, Daddy—'

'Hugh,' the elderly Scot put in softly.

She gave him a grateful smile. 'Hugh is completely right, Daddy,' she corrected. 'You have no reason to move to Majorca, certainly not to tell Peter that you've changed your mind about standing for parliament—'

'He most certainly does not,' Peter Ambrose was the one to put in strongly. 'And I wouldn't accept such a decision, either,' he added firmly. 'I need you, Paul.'

Her father looked pleased by these words of confidence. 'I don't want to be a liability—'

'You won't be,' Peter assured him with certainty. 'Hugh is quite right—I do have a place in mind for you in my proposed government.' He gave the elderly man a rueful smile for his insight. 'One that may involve a change of address,' he elaborated meaningfully.

'Well, now that's all settled, I think it's time Fergus and Chloe—'

'Really, Grandfather,' Fergus interrupted, 'don't you think you've interfered enough for one day?' He glared across at his grandfather.

'Not at all.' The elderly man was completely unperturbed by that glaring look. 'I'll have you know, I only interfered at all for your sake,' he stated enigmatically.

Chloe listened to the exchange between the two men in complete puzzlement. Oh, she agreed with Hugh; her father should not recant on his decision to go back into politics. There was absolutely no reason for him to do so. But where did she and Fergus come into that...?

More to the point, there was no Fergus and Chloe...!

'Somehow I find that hard to believe,' Fergus snapped angrily. 'And maybe if you had asked me first—'

'I did,' Hugh came back completely unrepentantly. 'But I have a wish to see my great-grandchildren before I'm in my grave—not have you bring them along to visit me afterwards!'

Chloe was completely lost now. In truth, she was still so stunned by this evening's revelations, she couldn't think straight, let alone make sense of Fergus's conversation with his grandfather.

There were a few things she had no doubts about, though—David's secret had remained exactly that for eight years, and should continue to do so. It would serve no purpose for it ever to be otherwise. Also her father must continue with his initial plan to stand for parliament.

She would move to Paris within the next few weeks...

'Grandfather, you really are an interfering old—'

'Now then, lad,' Hugh cut off Fergus's outburst. 'Remember we're in company,' he admonished. 'If you don't ask her, I will,' he declared tauntingly, before turning to Chloe's father. 'Paul, do you have a garden in which Fergus can walk with your daughter?'

Her father looked as dazed by the conversation as Chloe did. And of course they had a garden, but besides the fact she had no wish to walk in it at the moment, she didn't think Fergus had, either!

'Of course we do,' her mother was the one to answer warmly. 'Penny, darling, show Fergus the way out into the garden. Chloe, go with him,' she directed with unusual firmness.

It was the fact that it was so unusual for her mother to be so firm that Chloe went. At least, that was what she told herself...

Fergus had no such excuse, but he followed Chloe and Penny out into the hallway, too.

Penny turned and hugged her. 'I really am sorry that this has made things so difficult for you and Fergus,' she told Chloe emotionally. 'I really had no idea it was this serious between the two of you until Hugh told me... I don't think Mummy and Daddy did, either, until Hugh called to see them this afternoon, or Daddy would never have allowed it to have gone this far; he loves you equally as much as he loves me,' she said with certainty, squeezing Chloe's arm reassuringly before going back to join the other dinner guests.

Chloe was left standing in the hallway with Fergus, not quite knowing what to do next. At the moment she felt so embarrassed, first by what his grandfather had said, and now Penny, that she couldn't even look at him!

'My grandfather may be the interfering old goat I was going to accuse him of being just now,' Fergus spoke gruffly at her side. 'But his heart is in the right place. Whereas mine...' He paused. 'My heart is completely in your tender hands, Chloe Fox-Hamilton!'

Now she did look up at him, her eyes wide, feeling the colour fade and then rush back into her cheeks as she did so.

Because Fergus was looking at her with such love in his eyes she couldn't breathe...!

He reached out to gently clasp the top of her arm. 'Let's go and find that garden, hmm?' he suggested huskily.

Chloe led the way like an automaton. Had Fergus really just told her that his heart was hers...?

The perfume from the flowers outside was heady and strong, enough to make the senses reel. Except Chloe's were already reeling. Fergus loved her!

She found that incredible to believe. Still couldn't actually believe it.

'Chloe...?' Fergus was looking down at her uncertainly in the moonlight.

She moistened suddenly dry lips. 'I haven't been very nice to you the last couple of weeks,' she said inadequately.

He laughed softly. 'I'm not sure you've ever been that,' he acknowledged ruefully. 'But I live in hope.'

She swallowed hard. 'Is it true?'

'About David?' He frowned. 'I'm afraid so. But you mustn't blame him for the misconceptions over the identity of Susan Stirling's lover. He wanted to make a clean breast of it eight years ago and your father wouldn't let him, was determined to protect Penny and the children. And your father can be a very stubborn man—'

'No, not about David,' she corrected. 'I'm sure that's true. As I'm equally sure David and Penny now have one of the strongest marriages I know—apart from my parents, of course. But I—I was asking if it were true that you—that I—'

'That I love you?' Fergus finished gently. 'Oh, yes, Chloe, that's true.'

Her breath caught—and held—in her throat as she looked up at him. Fergus was looking at her with such all-consuming love in his face that she couldn't doubt how he felt about her.

Could it be, could it possibly be, after these past weeks of misunderstanding and pain, that everything was going to turn out all right after all…?

'I tried so hard to make everything all right again for you,' Fergus confessed 'But all I ever seemed to succeed in doing was hurting you more. But I really did try, Chloe. Please believe me.'

She did believe him, didn't need him to tell her any more about that. The past was well and truly gone; it was the future that mattered. A future with Fergus...?

'Fergus, I love you,' she spoke breathlessly.

'You do?' He looked as stunned as she must have done a few minutes ago when he'd told her his heart was hers.

She laughed softly, elated happiness starting to build up inside her. 'I do.'

'Enough to marry me?'

'Only if you're sure that's what you want.' Her expression betrayed her own uncertainty with this suggestion. Loving her was one thing, marrying her was something else entirely...

He reached out to wrap his arms about the slenderness of her waist. 'If you really do love me, then I wouldn't settle for anything less,' he assured her.

Chloe felt her heart leap in her chest. 'Oh, I really do love you,' she told him.

His arms tightened about her. 'Then—Chloe Fox-Hamilton, will you do me the honour of becoming my wife?'

Chloe slid her arms about his waist, resting her head against his chest, able to hear the erratic beating of his heart as he waited for her answer. 'I would love to,' she answered him emotionally.

The next moment she found herself swept off her feet as Fergus lifted her into his arms and carried her over to the wooden bench that stood in one corner of the garden, sitting down with her safely on his knees before his mouth claimed hers.

All the misunderstandings, all the pain, all the unhappiness, of the last few weeks, were swept away in the total honesty of their kisses. They were unable to get enough of each other, Chloe's fingers entwined in Fergus's hair as she kissed him with all the love that burnt inside her for him.

Their faces were flushed, eyes shining brightly, when they at last broke the kiss to simply gaze at each other.

Fergus reached up a hand to gently touch one of her flushed cheeks. 'I can hardly believe you're going to be my wife,' he murmured huskily.

Chloe smiled at him a little shyly, still overwhelmed by the love between them. 'Especially as a wife was the last thing you had on your mind only a few weeks ago!'

It had happened so quickly, this love between them, had taken them both by surprise. But even now, only a few minutes into knowing they loved each other, Chloe also knew she never wanted to be without Fergus in her life. She hoped he felt the same way...

Fergus's arms tightened about her. 'If I'm completely honest—and in future, I intend being completely that where you're concerned,' he stated forcefully, 'I think marriage has been on my mind from the moment I woke up on that Sunday morning and found you standing beside my bed!' he admitted. 'And I've never deliberately gone out of my way to avoid marriage—until now I've just never met the one woman I know I simply can't live without.'

'Oh, Fergus...!' she groaned ecstatically as she buried her face in the warmth of his throat. 'That's exactly what I wanted to hear!'

His arms tightened about her. 'I love you very much, Chloe, and I intend telling you so every day of our lives together,' he promised.

Chloe hadn't known such all-consuming happiness existed until this moment, knew now exactly why her father and mother, and Penny and David, had fought so hard to keep their marriage alive and healthy. Love like this was simply too precious to ever give up.

Fergus looked at her quizzically. 'Exactly when do we move to Paris?'

Her eyes widened in surprise. 'We? But—'

'You don't think I'm letting you go without me, do you?' Fergus raised dark brows. 'All those romantic Parisians paying court to you?' He shook his head firmly. 'I don't think so. Besides, I'm an author, I can write anywhere. Paris sounds as good a place as any.'

Chloe couldn't believe he was really willing to do this for her... 'It will only be for a few months...'

'An extended honeymoon.' Fergus nodded with satisfaction. 'I can hardly wait! You do realise, after all his machinations, that we'll probably have to name our first child after my grandfather,' he added teasingly. 'Hugh McCloud.' He grimaced.

'Let's hope it's a girl.' Chloe giggled happily. She didn't care what they called their first child, the fact that it would be a product of the love they shared would be enough.

Fergus became serious again. 'Marry me soon,' he urged gruffly. 'Very soon.'

'Yes, please,' she accepted ecstatically.

He smiled at her warmly. 'Do you think we ought to go in now and put them all out of their misery?' he teased.

Chloe sobered briefly. 'I think there has been quite enough misery this last few weeks.'

'Then it's time for some celebrating instead,' Fergus decided firmly, sliding her gently off his knee as he stood up, but still retaining a hold of one of her hands. 'Let's go and open up some champagne—and invite everyone to a wedding!' he announced with satisfaction.

A sentiment Chloe was only too happy to agree with!

CHAPTER FIFTEEN

'OH, FERGUS, isn't this just wonderful?' Chloe exclaimed happily at his side. 'I'm so happy I want to cry,' she added emotionally.

'Hormones, my love,' Fergus drawled indulgently, although he knew it wasn't just Chloe's two-month pregnancy that made her so weepy; today really was a wonderful day for them all.

But especially for Chloe's father. Yesterday he and his political party had achieved a landslide victory in the general election, and today Peter Ambrose had asked Paul to be Chancellor of the Exchequer.

The party had started a couple of hours ago at the home of Chloe's parents, and looked like going on well into the evening and night, all the family here, including Fergus's, and many other people from the world of business and politics.

He and Chloe had been married for six months now, had returned from Chloe's successful Paris show only last month, and Fergus knew they had been the happiest six months of his life. Now, with Chloe's pregnancy confirmed only this morning, that happiness was totally overwhelming.

'I love you, Chloe,' he told her huskily.

'And I love you,' she returned as emotionally.

Fergus knew it was all he wanted. All he would ever want.

'When shall we tell them our news?' Chloe looked up excitedly at her husband, her breath catching in her throat just to know that the two of them were so happy together.

'Whenever you like,' Fergus replied indulgently. 'Personally, I want to shout it to the whole world!'

That was exactly how she felt, and she never ceased to be amazed that this wonderful man loved her as deeply as she loved him.

'At least we won't have to call him Hugh now.' She grinned with a wistful look across the room at Darcy and Logan as they cooed over their newborn son, Daniel Hugh.

'He may be a she,' Fergus returned teasingly. 'But I know what you mean.'

He usually did. That was the strange—and wonderful!—thing about marriage; the two of them were totally attuned to each other's thoughts and feelings.

'Poor Brice,' Chloe murmured as she looked across the room to where her cousin-in-law stood alone in one of the bay windows, surveying the party through remote green eyes. 'He needs someone in his life too,' she explained at Fergus's questioning look.

Fergus chuckled, shaking his head derisively. 'Brice is perfectly capable of finding someone if he wants to.'

'But he may not know he wants to,' Chloe reasoned.

Fergus laughed softly as he turned her in the circle of his arms. 'Never mind what Brice does or doesn't want,' he said. 'How soon do you think we can leave?' His eyes darkened to chocolate-brown. 'I have a burning desire to make love to my wife!'

Chloe knew that same desire, and after six months of marriage she knew that she always would.

She and Fergus had a love that would last for ever...

MILLS & BOON® PUBLISH EIGHT LARGE PRINT TITLES A MONTH. THESE ARE THE EIGHT TITLES FOR NOVEMBER 2002

THE BRIDAL BARGAIN
Emma Darcy

THE TYCOON'S VIRGIN
Penny Jordan

TO MARRY McCLOUD
Carole Mortimer

MISTRESS OF LA RIOJA
Sharon Kendrick

STRATEGY FOR MARRIAGE
Margaret Way

THE TYCOON'S TAKEOVER
Liz Fielding

THE HONEYMOON PRIZE
Jessica Hart

HER FORBIDDEN BRIDEGROOM
Susan Fox

MILLS & BOON®

1002 Rom LP

MILLS & BOON® PUBLISH EIGHT LARGE PRINT TITLES A MONTH. THESE ARE THE EIGHT TITLES FOR DECEMBER 2002

THE HONEYMOON CONTRACT
Emma Darcy

ETHAN'S TEMPTRESS BRIDE
Michelle Reid

HIS CONVENIENT MARRIAGE
Sara Craven

THE ITALIAN'S TROPHY MISTRESS
Diana Hamilton

THE FIANCÉ FIX
Carole Mortimer

BRIDE BY DESIGN
Leigh Michaels

THE WHIRLWIND WEDDING
Day Leclaire

HER MARRIAGE SECRET
Darcy Maguire

MILLS & BOON®